George Radley

SHORT LIFE AND OTHER STORIES

AUSTIN MACAULEY PUBLISHERS™

LONDON • CAMBRIDGE • NEW YORK • SHARJAH

A CIP catalogue record for this title is available from the British Library.

ISBN 9781035870462 (Paperback)
ISBN 9781035870486 (ePub e-book)

www.austinmacauley.com

First Published 2023
Austin Macauley Publishers Ltd®
1 Canada Square
Canary Wharf
London
E14 5AA

To all the people who supported my first book. Thanks for
giving it a review and recommending it to
your family and friends.

Table of Contents

Short Story 1
Bad Karma
Page 1

Dave and Phil came rushing out the Acorns Charity shop, both laughing. They pushed past an elderly woman going in.

"That was a bit of luck," said Dave.

"Yes, I couldn't believe it when that woman left her purse on the bookcase," replied Phil.

"I think she was going to check to see how much money she had when her phone went off."

"I quickly slipped it into my pocket when no one was looking. The woman was too engrossed in her phone call to notice me," said Phil.

"Let's go back to your place and check to see what's in it."

Later on, they discovered that there was £100 in there, a debit card and a credit card.

Phil and Dave were former workmates at a factory which had shut down six months ago. They had struggled to get work since and were having to survive on benefits. Both were in their mid-30s. Phil was taller than Dave at over six feet and quite slim. He was more extrovert and reckless than Dave, who was quieter and more thoughtful.

"Let's go to the city centre to see if there are any little old ladies with purses on the top of their bags," stated Phil.

"Are you sure that's a good idea? It's not a good thing to do," replied Dave.

"We're short of money and we won't hurt them." said Phil not too convincingly.

"OK but let's think of other ways to get money," replied Dave. While in the Bull Ring Shopping Centre, on the crowded escalators they managed to steal another two purses, without anyone noticing.

"Let's go to Aldi. I need to buy some food for tonight," said Dave.

"Let's make its Marks and Spencer's. I have a new shoplifting system to try out," replied Phil.

"All right. You will have to show me."

While in Marks and Spencer's, Phil showed Dave his new way of shoplifting.

"You get a basket and put your carrier bag; a quarter full of items in the bottom of the basket and leave the bag open. Then you go around putting food and other items in the basket but you put most of the items in the bag and the rest in the basket," said Phil.

"That sounds a clever way of doing it," stated Dave.

"Then when you have the bag three quarters full, take it out of the basket and hold it. Then go and pay for the few items in the basket."

"Won't someone see your bag?" said Dave.

"Yes, but they will think you bought the food somewhere else. Nobody will check your bag," stated Phil.

"Then when you pay for your goods, make sure that they are the cheapest ones you get, you add them to your three quarters full bag," added Phil.

This seemed to work. No one challenged Phil or Dave at the till or on the way out.

"I reckon we got away with about £40 worth of food there. My system works better at shops like Marks and Spencer's because there are less people there than at Aldi, or The Co-op."

"It works very well. We've had a good day today," replied Dave.

"Yes. It's Saturday tomorrow, shall we meet up again in the afternoon? I want to visit that new charity shop, British Heart Foundation, in Birmingham," said Phil.

"All right, say 2 pm outside the Charity shop," replied Dave.

The next day Dave met up with Phil outside The British Heart Foundation Charity Shop, just after 2 pm.

"Hi Mate," said Dave.

"Hi Dave. Let's go inside. I could do with some trousers and some T-shirts."

"How are you going to nick them?"

"I shall wait until it's busy, take in several items of clothes into the changing room and then nick most of them," replied Phil.

"All right, let's go inside and see what they have."

Inside the shop they separated. Phil went to look at the men's clothes while Dave browsed through the CDs. After ten minutes Phil took several items of clothes into the changing room.

He waited until the volunteer at the till was busy.

When Phil was in the changing room he quickly went to work. He had taken five items in there even though the maximum was three. He put the three most expensive items in his bag, two pairs of jeans and a shirt. Then he tried on a cheap T-shirt he intended to buy, which fitted him. After doing this Phil came out of the changing room, put one T-shirt back on the rail and then bought the cheap T-shirt for £1.99. He then went out the shop to wait for Dave.

Meanwhile Dave was busy stealing CDs. He took out a CD he liked, slipped it in his carrier bag and then put the empty cover back on display. He managed to steal six CDs in this way.

Then he had a quick look at a few other items before casually leaving the shop. Outside he met up with Phil.

"How did it go?"

"Really well," said Phil. "I nicked two pairs of jeans and one T-shirt. They were marked up as £4.99, £4.99 and £1.99 so I saved nearly £12 and got some good quality clothes."

"Where did you put the hangers?"

"I left most of them on the rails and only took in one hanger for the cheap T-shirt I bought. It saves me having to hide the hangers in the changing room. What did you get?"

"I did quite well, nicking six CDs. They are good quality ones, Joy Division, The Stranglers, Radiohead, The Kinks, The Smiths and The Specials," replied Dave.

"What about covers?"

"I have some old ones at home. I can put them in those."

"All right, we are on a roll. What about a couple more charity shops before going home? I need a good jacket, a good pair of trousers and a good shirt, which I can hopefully wear to job interviews," said Phil.

OK, let's try Age UK and Barnado's.

So, Phil used the same tactics as before and managed to get two quality jackets, three good pairs of black trousers and three shirts. Dave just browsed and kept an eye on the shop's volunteers and managers. Afterwards they met up and walked to Phil's car to go home.

"These charity shops are easy to steal from; it's like robbing a disabled person," stated Phil.

"You're right. The volunteers are so trusting. They don't suspect us because we are, reasonably well dressed and fairly respectable. They are too busy watching the young kids," replied Dave.

"Yes, we can sneak in under the radar," said Phil, laughing.

"Let's go home and drop our things off. We can meet up later for a drink," said Dave.

"All right we can meet up at 8 pm in the Kings Head pub."

Later they both met up and had a few drinks. They left at about 11.30 pm. While outside the pub, Phil checked his phone to read a text someone had sent him. Suddenly, a young kid appeared from nowhere and snatched the phone from his hand and ran off to a waiting car.

Phil and Dave were so surprised they didn't react quickly enough. The car sped off.

"F--k it!" said Phil, loudly.

"Damn thief!" shouted Dave.

"That was a bloody good phone, the latest one."

"What are you going to do?" enquired Dave.

"We can't do much about it now. Let's see if we can get another one tomorrow. I could pick you up at 11 am."

"OK. See you tomorrow," replied Dave.

Dave didn't stay up too long when he reached home. It was nearly midnight so he went to bed. He had a disturbed night. He had a bad dream about someone chasing him and another one, more worryingly, about his dad. His dad had died a few years earlier and had been a committed Christian and he wasn't too pleased about something. He looked angry and shook his fist at Dave. It unnerved him.

He awoke suddenly at 4.30 am. He thought he heard a noise. Dave lived alone in a one bedroomed flat on the ground floor of a house. There was only one other tenant in the house, who had the next floor up but he was on holiday. Had he come back early?

Dave lay there trembling, listening for any sound. It was quiet for about two minutes before he heard more noise. It was very close, possibly his living room. He slowly climbed out of bed, put on his trousers, found a torch and quietly approached the door. He opened it quietly and shone his torch in the room. There were two men carrying out his computer. He shouted out. They dropped it and ran out the door. Dave put the light on and was shocked to see what a mess the room was in. The cushions from his settee and chairs had been thrown on the floor. Some of his CDs and DVDs were scattered on the floor. Most had been stolen.

There weren't many left.

After tidying up for two hours, his living room looked much better. He checked to see what was taken. It was a lot of items, his LG television set, his CD player, radio cassette player and lots of CDs And DVDs. Also strangely enough were his two bars of chocolate, which he was looking forward to having later.

Dave checked to see how they had got in. They had broken a window in the living room and climbed in to open the door. He decided not to report it to the police. They rarely caught burglars and he also wasn't insured.

At 11am Phil called for Dave and they went for a drink in a nearby pub.

"What has happened to your car?" said Dave.

"It was nicked during the night. I didn't hear anything."

"Sorry to hear about that. I have had bad luck as well. I was broken into in the early hours of the morning."

"Have you had much taken?"

"Yeah, loads of stuff. My TV, Radio Cassette Player, lots of CD's and DVDs. No money though but that's because I haven't got much." replied Dave.

"It looks like we have both had bad luck," stated Phil.

"Is it bad luck though? Could it be karma?"

"What do you mean?" said a puzzled Phil.

"I think it's down to bad karma. It works like this. If you do good things the universe rewards you but if you do bad things, the universe punishes you."

"I've heard of it before but do you believe in it?"

"I wasn't so sure before but think about it we have been robbing charity shops and stealing women's purses. It's not good is it?" stated Dave.

"No, but we did have an agreement that we would do what we could to get by, including stealing things, until we found jobs."

"I know but we have gone too far. A bit of shop lifting at Marks and Spencer's and other big stores isn't so bad because they won't really miss the money but we shouldn't be stealing from charity shops and vulnerable people."

"We have been struggling to get jobs and the job seekers money is not enough. We didn't hurt anybody. What can we do?" replied Phil.

"I've been thinking about it. I know we both don't like work agencies because of the zero contract hours but I think we should join one to see how it goes. It could keep us going until we can get full time jobs." stated Dave.

"Are you sure?" said Phil.

"Remember our former workmate, George. He joined a work agency and prospered. He's now a Team Leader," added Dave.

"All right. We'll sign up to a work agency tomorrow. I've heard that People Line aren't too bad."

Six months later after getting regular work at a company while working for People Line, the company took them both on as permanent workers.

Short Story 2
The Fake Call
Page 1

I was on my way over to see my friend Tom in Wolverhampton. We were going to watch a Premiership football game on Sky at a pub in the city centre, a friendly place where it didn't get too rowdy. I had travelled there by bus which took me about one hour. I passed the time by reading a newspaper. I enjoyed reading so I didn't mind the long journey. Tom was already there when I arrived. He lived quite close so he didn't have too far to travel. Tom was 41 years old, medium size build and had fair hair. He was quite good looking and always had more good luck with women than I had. Even though I was a similar age and slimmer and in better shape I had always struggled to get a girlfriend whereas Tom could find one so easily. Maybe I was a bit more introverted and less outgoing. It might also have been because Tom had a better paid job and was richer than me.

After buying a drink I went over to sit down and chat with him. He looked depressed and down.

"How are things?" I said.

"Not too good, Tracy is getting on my nerves. I wish she would go."

Tracy was his girlfriend. They had been together for 3 years but it hadn't been going that well recently. They hadn't got much in common and Tracy's irritating habits had finally got to him.

"You have told her that it isn't working haven't you?" I said.

"Yes but she doesn't listen. She doesn't want to break up. She won't take no for an answer."

"1 did warn you that she wasn't that interesting and hadn't got too much in common with you."

"1 know but she is very attractive. She's got a nice figure, she's blonde and she dresses well. I couldn't resist her," stated Tom.

"1 suppose that's the difference between you and me. I wouldn't have found her interesting enough to have gone out with her. Also she's not the cleverest woman you have been out with."

"Mind you she did ask me out." said Tom laughing.

"Oh, I had forgotten. Why do women never ask me out?"

"You need to be more confident. Women like confident men."

"It's awkward because she lives with you in your flat."

"I can't force her to go or throw her things out," complained Tom.

"I shall try to find a solution for you," I said.

"OK. Thanks. I will be grateful."

We settled down to watch the game. It turned out to be a high scoring game. Tom was pleased because his team won. It took his mind off his 'girlfriend problem.'

On the bus home, I thought about Tom's problem with his girlfriend and tried to find a way to help him. Tom had been a good friend to me. He had helped me through a tough time recently, one of the few people to have helped me so I wanted to give him some help. Before I reached home I had an idea. Tracy was claiming Disability Benefit even though there wasn't that much wrong with her. She was just a bit overweight as far as I could see. She had put on a couple of stones in the last year but was still reasonably attractive. Tracy should be living with her mom, who was designated as her carer but lived permanently with Tom.

I thought I could exploit this situation by pretending to be an official from the Department of Work and Pensions (D.W.P) and warn her that she could lose her benefit. I was good at accents so I could disguise my voice. I thought I could use my best South African accent. My name would be David Pieterson. I would have to ask Tom to agree to this. When I texted Tom about my plan he agreed to it immediately. I could tell he was desperate to finish with Tracy.

I asked Tom for some details about Tracy, her full name, her mom's address, what type of disability allowance she was claiming and whether Tracy's mom was her designated carer, which she was. He texted me the answers. We also agreed on the day and the time for this 'official phone call.' This would be tomorrow morning, Monday. I would do it before I went to work on my afternoon shift.

Before I went to bed, I wrote down a list of question to ask her. I had to be prepared. I was nervous but reasonably confident.

I got up the next morning at 10am, had a drink and got my list of questions out. I read through them to familiarise myself with them. I then steadied my nerves and took the plunge.

I used my landline phone and rang Tom's number. He answered it and I adopted a strong South African accent.

"Can I speak to Tracy Edwards please?"

"Yes. I will get her," replied Tom.

"Hello, who's calling?" said Tracy with a quivering voice.

"This is David Pieterson from the Department of Work and Pensions, I have reason to believe that you are living full time with your boyfriend, Tom Hadley. Is that correct?"

"Er. no," said Tracy shakily.

"We have been monitoring you and we are 100% certain that you are living there," I stated.

"No, I just visit him occasionally and stay overnight sometimes."

"I'm afraid you are not telling the truth Miss Edwards. I am legally required to give you a warning. If you don't return to your mother's house, your benefit will be stopped until we work out your new smaller benefit."

"You can't do that, can you?" answered Tracy.

"Yes, we can. We know that your mom is registered as your carer so this means you should be living full time with your mother, not visiting her a few times a week."

Tracy went quiet. I could hear her whispering to Tom what I said.

Then she returned to the phone.

"What office do you work at?" she said, going on the attack.

"The Birmingham office," I replied.

Then she threw me. I had anticipated most of her replies and questions but didn't expect this question.

"What is the number of your office? I want to speak to your manager," said Tracy.

I panicked a bit and just made up any Birmingham number that came into my head.

I then told her that I had to finish because I had another important call to make. I hurriedly hung up. I had told Tom that as soon as I had finished talking to Tracy to ring his own number so my number wasn't the last number on his phone. It had gone fairly well until right at the end when I had to make up a number. I found out later that Tracy had rung this number while at her mom's house and discovered that the number was that of a female escorts number, which made me laugh.

Two hours later Tom texted me to say that Tracy had panicked after the call and had arranged for her sister to collect her straight away in her car to take her back to her mom's house. Tracy had hurriedly packed a couple of bags of clothes and other items. It had worked. She had gone.

Tom texted me again later that evening to say that Tracy had contacted him and said she would stay at her Mom's house for a few months and lie low until things had quietened down. He thanked me.

The next time I saw Tom he looked like a different person. He was happy, laughing and joking. He told me he hadn't seen Tracy move so fast after my 'fake DWP call'. $he was like a kid rushing to go to the ice cream van.

"Are you going to see her again?" I asked.

"No. I told her the next day that it's best if we finish seeing each other."

"How did she take it?"

"Not too well." replied Tom.

"You are doing the right thing. It's best to make a clean break with her now she's left your flat."

"Yes. You're right. Now let me buy you a drink for helping me get rid of her."

"Can I have some champagne?" I said laughing.

Short Story 3
Short Life
Page 1

My name is Galina and I am the leader of my herd, the dominant male Bull Elephant. I am 12 feet tall, weigh 5 tonnes and I am full of bulging muscle. I have been the leader of my herd for four years now and I am in my prime, at 25 years old.

Despite all this strength and muscle I am quite a soft hearted elephant really. I don't throw my weight around and I rule with a soft touch, especially with the younger male elephants. I can be tough when I want to be towards any troublesome outsiders or any uppity young bull elephants who want to take my place. I usually glare at them and trumpet loudly at any cocky young male elephant who does try it on. They soon go scurrying off. I am in my prime and I am not going anywhere yet!

We live in The Sambura National Reserve in Kenya. It's a beautiful place with a large forest and the Ewaso Rugiro river running through it, but it's also a tough place to live. At certain times of the year there are droughts and we have to trek for miles to another watering hole. Thankfully we are vegetarians and we don't have to kill other animals to survive.

In spite of our size we do have some predators. Many wild dogs, hyenas and lions can kill our baby calves if we are not careful. Also some desperately hungry lions can attack full grown elephants. I have to be on my guard when there are lions in the area.

An even bigger predator than lions is man, the kind with shotguns. I know not all humans are bad. The Park Rangers we have in this reserve are very caring and look out for us as much as they can. Also tourists don't wish us any harm. There are, however, some nasty men around who are greedy and ruthless, killing us just for our tusks to make silly ornaments or to make Chinese medicines.

The numbers of our species worries me. Our numbers go down every year, mainly through the hunting of us for ivory. My life span is 70 but I doubt if I shall reach it. Some of my herd have already been killed by these poachers.

As well as poaching, men build villages on our land, land we have roamed on for centuries. Then they complain when we trample through their crops. Why should we have to go around their villages and farms? Maybe man needs to cut his population and stop encroaching on our ancient lands.

During the night, there is lots of noise; shooting,

shouting and cars speeding off. The next morning, I hear from Amora, one of the younger elephants, that poachers had tried to attack our herd but the Rangers had fought them off. This worries me because poachers are in the area and they won't want to leave without getting some ivory. The price of our ivory is so high that it is worth the risk for these poachers. As the biggest elephant in the herd I am the main target. I shall have to be watchful and very careful now.

It's early morning so we all go down to the water hole. I go first to check to see if it's safe for everyone. There are the usual animals, giraffes, zebras, hippos and Grant's gazelles. No lions. No crocodiles. No threats. It's safe so I call them over by trumpeting to them with my trunk. They all hurry over to drink thirstily, filling their trunks with water. After we have quenched our thirst, we move away to a safer area.

Afterwards most of us eat on the abundant grass and trees, while the younger males play fight with each other. This scene looks so peaceful and happy but the knowledge that poachers are in the area still worries me. I think about moving away but these poachers always find us. We can't go anywhere without them catching up with us eventually.

It's dark now and everyone is getting ready to sleep. We elephants don't sleep much anyway but I can't sleep tonight at all. I walk around nervously. I check that everyone is safe.

Soon everyone is sleeping. I wonder around in a nervous state, putting my big ears to use by listening to every sound. I can even hear a vole moving through the grass.

Then I hear a louder rustle. What is that? I listen again, more rustling. This is no vole. It's the poachers. I start to panic. My heart starts beating very fast. I don't want them to go near the rest of the herd. They have come for me. I decide to move away from the rest. I hurry away to where there are some trees, hoping I might be able to hide behind them.

While there I realise, I have no chance. I can take on another bull elephant, a crocodile and even a lion but I can't deal with a man with a gun.

I can now smell them. Then I see them. There are three men, our biggest predator. One is aiming the gun at me. I start to run. I am big but I can run fast when necessary. I run but I run straight into another two men. They have ambushed me.

I feel the first bullet hit my head. Wow, the pain is incredible! Then the second bullet hits me in the side. The third bullet hits me in the head again. Blood starts pouring down me. I fall to the ground in agony.

Then suddenly the pain goes. I see my life flash before me. I see myself being born, then in my carefree youth, playing with my brother. After that fighting another bull elephant and beating him, mating with Echo and finally leading my herd.

I have lived out my life. I am only 25 years old. I think of my herd, of Echo. I don't want to leave them. I don't want to die.

I console myself with the thought that some part of me will live on, someone's shelf.

Short Story 4
Revenge Is a Dish Best Served Cold
Page 1

It was good to be back home again. I had just returned from a great, one week holiday to the Lake District with my mom and brother, Mike. It was one of my favourite places in Britain, a picturesque place full of beautiful lakes and hills. We all had a relaxing time there enjoying the lovely scenery, going on walks, reading and visiting several interesting places on days out.

Mike dropped me off at my flat. Then he and my mom headed off to my mom's house, a few roads away. I was intending to put my things away, have a shower and a change of clothes before going back to my mom's house for an evening meal.

I made my way down the entry, unlocking both entry gates. Then I made my way to the front door. I stopped suddenly… the door was open!

"Oh no!" I said aloud. I rushed over and went inside. It was my worst nightmare. My flat had been broken into. "Damn it!" I shouted.

I went into my bedroom. It was a right mess. The mattress had been overturned and the sheets were all over the floor. Clothes from my wardrobe had also been thrown onto the floor. The chest of drawers had also been ransacked.

Next, I went into the bathroom. The airing cupboard with all my towels in had been searched, resulting in all my towels being thrown onto the floor.

My living room was just as bad. The cushions from the settee and the two armchairs had been thrown onto the floor. Again, this room was in a right mess.

This is what a lot of people, who haven't been burgled don't understand. It's not just the items stolen that matter but the mess these thieves make while searching for valuable things. They don't care about your possessions, many of which could be of sentimental value. They throw them everywhere and sometimes smash things.

I looked to see how they had got in. My flat is a long and narrow garden flat. It has windows in the bedroom, bathroom, kitchen and living room, all on the long side of the flat. In addition, there is another window in the living room, which is on the end part of the flat, close to the back garden at the back. This was the window that the thieves had broken into. A large crowbar lay on the floor by the window. They had got in through this window because it wasn't visible from next door or the other three flats in the main house.

I then looked to see what had been stolen. Surprisingly enough my television was still there, although it wasn't a modern type. The DVD player had been taken, along with my radio cassette player. After a further inspection of my flat I noticed all my large albums, in three cases, had gone. I didn't play them these days. I only kept them because of sentimental value and because some covers were so good, such as The Beatles 'Sergeant Pepper's Lonely Hearts Club Band' album.

I hadn't kept any money in the place and I am not the type of person who has much jewellery, especially expensive watches. I hadn't lost that much. I had got away with it really.

I phoned my mom to say I would be late for tea because of my break-in. She was horrified and said she would be over straight away to help me clean up. I also phoned my landlord to inform him of the situation. He said he was sorry to hear about it and would try to visit soon.

Finally, I phoned the police to report the burglary. They said they would visit me tomorrow. I didn't think there was any chance of them catching the thieves so I started to clean up.

My mom joined me soon after and we tidied up, putting everything back in its place. She was shocked at the mess but between us we managed to get it looking reasonably clean and tidy. I put the sheets and the duvet cover out for washing and replaced them with a spare duvet cover and clean sheets that my mom had brought up. Finally, my mom vacuumed up all the rooms. I thanked her for her help. It was good of her to come and help me because I didn't feel like doing it all myself. I appreciated her help. Later we both went back to her house to have some dinner. My brother was also there and we talked a lot about the break-in.

The next day I thought about who could have broken in. There were two locks on the gates, one at the front of the entry and one at the end, leading into the garden and my flat. I don't believe anyone outside would have got in. The gates were six feet high and quite solid. The next-door neighbours, who also shared this entry were a respectable couple. They always acknowledged me when they saw me. I don't believe it was them.

There were three separate flats in the main house. All had access and keys to the back garden so they could put rubbish in the dustbin and recycled items in the recycling bins.

Could it be one of them? The top floor flat had a nice couple living there. I don't think it was them. The second floor flat had a middle-aged man living there on his own. Not him.

"Wait a minute," I said aloud. The first floor had a fairly dodgy character, called Dean, living there, a young man in his mid-twenties. He was a bit rough and unfriendly. I had never really got on with him. Could it be him? I thought it must be someone in these flats because the break-in occurred when I was on holiday for a week. It was too much of a coincidence for it to be someone from outside.

All these three flats had fire escapes so they didn't even need to go around the back but just go down the fire escape, which was very handy for a thief.

Later in the afternoon two policemen visited. I showed them where the thief broke in and the crowbar they had used. One examined the window for fingerprints but couldn't find any. The thief had used gloves. The police gave me a crime number so I could give it to my insurance company, which I didn't have as I couldn't afford the insurance. They also took the crowbar away to have it checked for fingerprints. Even though I had marked most of my stuff with my postcode and name, I didn't expect them to find the thief and retrieve my things.

A week later, I was on my way back home from work on a Friday evening when I saw Dean and his friend leaving his flat. They were probably going to the local pub. I went down the entry to go to my flat. As I was about to go into my flat, I looked up and noticed Dean's bedroom window was open. It had been hot recently and everyone had been leaving their windows open. He had forgotten to shut it before going out.

A thought suddenly came to me. It was a mad idea. I thought about going in his flat to look around. He was the chief suspect as far as I could see. I thought quickly.

It was nearly 8 pm and it was getting dark. I looked at my next-door neighbours. Their curtains were drawn. I decided to take a risk. I put on some gloves and climbed up the fire escape quietly.

When I reached Dean's window, I called out to him quietly just in case he had returned unexpectedly. I could make up a story about seeing his window open and climbing up the fire escape to warn him that he could be burgled. Thankfully he wasn't there.

I quickly got to work. I searched all his rooms for any signs of my items. I couldn't find the DVD Player or the radio cassette player but I did see my three cases of albums at the bottom of his wardrobe. So, Dean was the thief. He probably couldn't find a buyer for the albums yet.

I thought about what to do. I had a look out of the window to see if there was any sign of dodgy Dean. No sign of him. I couldn't take them back because he would know it was me.

An idea came to me, look under his mattress. Under here there were dozens of packets of drugs, cocaine and cannabis. *Got you* I thought. I carefully put the mattress back in place and made sure I left everything the same as I found it. I didn't worry too much because the place wasn't too clean. Dodgy Dean was a messy person. Typical of most young men today. His bedroom had lots of clothes scattered on the floor and his kitchen sink had several dirty mugs and plates in it. Even if I had left some things in a mess he wouldn't have noticed.

I had another look out the window. Still no sign of dodgy Dean so I quietly crept down the stairs of the fire escape and out into the back garden. No one was about. It was silent. I then made my way back to my flat.

The next day I made an anonymous phone call to Crime Stoppers to inform them that Dean was a small-time drug dealer, that he had drugs in his flat and also that he was responsible for most of the burglaries in the area in the last few months.

It took a few weeks but the police eventually raided his flat and arrested him. As I had written my name and postcode on the albums, I got them back. Sometimes good things happen from bad things. I was broken into but it resulted in a drug dealer and thief being put away for four years. As that old saying goes: 'Revenge is a dish best served cold.'

Short Story 5

Dateline

Page 1

I clicked on the dating website, Partners, and looked at many of the female profiles on the site. Most seemed to be attractive, respectable and of varying ages, including my age group, 45. It seemed a good dating website. I filled in my profile, paid my fee and uploaded a few of my better photos of myself. One was of me on Clent Hills showing how fit and active I was. Another was of me with my sister's pet cat, showing my caring side and my love of animals.

I had decided to try an online dating website because my best friend, Will, had some success. He had been out with several interesting women and had finally met his current girlfriend, Sandie, on there. I remember him telling me about this when we met up for a drink at my local pub a few weeks ago, on a Saturday night.

"Why don't you give it a try, Gary?" said Will.

"You mean online dating?" I replied.

"Yes. It's worked for me."

"Didn't you meet a few odd women on there?"

"Yes, early on there were a few strange ones. They contacted me. I replied to some of them but I didn't like the sound of them."

"What was the name of the first woman you went out with?" I asked.

"Donna. I contacted her. She was attractive, tall, slim and blonde. I went out with her for a couple of weeks but I finished with her."

"Why was that?"

"She drank too much, too much of everything, wine, vodka, lager and spirits. You wouldn't think it when you meet her for the first time. She's from a fairly rich, middle-class family."

"I remember you going out with that nice looking brunette for a while," I said.

"Yes, that was Emma."

"What happened to her?" I enquired.

"She dumped me after about three dates."

"Why was that?"

"She found a rich man on the dating site. I can't compete with a millionaire businessman. Mind you I didn't mind because I found Sandie." said Will.

"She's very nice. You've got lucky with her."

"Yes, you're right. She's a lovely woman. I would like us to keep on seeing each other." stated Will.

"That's good. I'm thinking of joining the same dating site but I 'm worried about con artists and fraudsters."

"I know what you mean. I did meet one woman who asked me for some money several times but I refused and she finally went away."

"I'm worried about meeting these types of people. Remember what happened to my sister, Jenny, a couple of years ago. She got scammed for £300." I added.

Later that night I checked this dating website to see if anyone had left a message for me.

There was only one message for me from a woman called Annabel. I clicked on her profile and I was staggered at how beautiful she was. Surely, she wouldn't have problems finding a man. I was intrigued by her. She was five feet seven inches tall, slim, blonde with blue eyes. Her interests almost matched mine. I decided to leave her a message along with a few photos.

An hour later Annabel had replied. She seemed eager to get to know me better and had left her phone number and email address to make it easier for us to contact each other. In addition she had sent me a few photos of herself. I replied immediately, telling her more things about me and enclosing more photos of myself.

When I went back to check my emails an hour later Annabel had replied to me and sent more photos of herself. These were very revealing, not exactly naked photos but ones of her wearing a short skirt, wearing stockings and suspenders and wearing a low-cut top. She left me a provocative message:

"Hi honey,

I hope you like these photos. There's more to come…
Love.
Annabel."

After I had looked at these photos, I thought something was not right. I had only contacted her that day and she had become too friendly.

An hour later another set of photos had been sent to me. My eyes nearly popped out of my head. They were all naked pictures of her. She had the body of a model. I didn't reply and soon after I went to bed. I dreamt about this woman all night.

The next day, Sunday, I eagerly went online to check my emails from Annabel. There was one. This time there were no sexy photos. Instead, there was a rushed, panicked email informing me of a problem. It read:

Hi Honey,

I'm very sorry to ask you but can you help me out. My mom is on holiday in America and she has had a serious accident. She is in hospital but she has to pay for her treatment. She doesn't have any insurance or any money to pay for her medical bill. She needs £500. I have to go out there soon to help her but I need to send her this money immediately. Can you please help me?

love
Annabel

I read this message in dismay. I thought things were going too well. I immediately suspected that this was a scam. I thought I would test her out. I emailed her and asked her why she couldn't ask her own family or friends for help, why she hasn't any money of her own and why she kept calling me honey and not my real name.

A couple of hours later I read her reply. She wrote:

Hi Honey,

Please believe me. I'm telling you the truth. I don't have any brothers and sisters and my dad left years ago and I'm not in contact with him. My friends don't have much money and can't help me. I don't have anyone to turn to except you. I only call people I love honey.

love
Annabel

After reading Annabel's latest email I then knew that she was lying and it was a potential scam. I thought about what to do. After about thirty minutes I had an idea. What about if I played along with her and pretended to help her? I could string her along by saying I would help her but delay it a lot and mess her about. I emailed her back, saying I could help her but I couldn't afford £500. I said I could just about manage £200.

Half an hour later she replied, stating that she needed it all. She said:

Hi Honey,

I need all of the money. American hospitals are expensive.

Love,

Annabel

I answered saying I would send it by bank transfer tomorrow, Monday. I asked her to send me her bank details, which she did. When Monday came, I emailed Annabel at around 11 am to tell her that I had tried to send her this money but there was a hold up at my bank and I couldn't do it. I told Annabel that three thieves had stormed into the bank demanding money and threatening the cashiers and customers. The female manager gave them all the money in the tills, over £10,000. All the customers, including myself were very frightened. The bank had to be closed for the day. I suggested I send her the money tomorrow morning. I said I had to go to work now. The story was made up but I tried to make it as convincing as I could and act upset. She seemed to believe my story and didn't question it.

On Tuesday morning, I emailed Annabel to inform her that I had misplaced my bank card and couldn't find it. I said that I had looked everywhere for it but had no luck finding it. I told her that I had to go to work for my afternoon shift but would look for it after work.

She replied by stating:

Hi Honey,

Please, please, please send me the money as soon as you can.

Love,
Annabel.

After work I replied that I found my card and I wouldn't let her down. I promised to send her the money early tomorrow morning, as soon as my bank was open, around 9 o'clock.

The next morning, I didn't send her the money in the morning and I didn't email her but went to work as usual. When I came back from work in the evening, I checked my emails on my computer and found that she had sent me six emails. They were all saying the same thing, where is the money? I answered by saying that I had woken up feeling terrible and I had the flu so I wouldn't be well for a few days. This caused Annabel to panic even more by saying that she was desperate for the money because the hospital in America were demanding the £500 before they would treat her mom. She needed the money tomorrow. I didn't reply to her that night.

I didn't reply to her for the next three days to make it look like I was really ill. Then I told her that I was better and I could now send her the money. During this time

Annabel had sent me about a dozen emails, all urging me to send her the money.

I waited for a reply but I didn't get one. She had got the message…

When I next spoke to Will he told me that he wasn't too surprised that Annabel was trying to scam me. He also reckoned that the reason Annabel kept calling me honey was because she was trying to con a lot of different men at the same time and that she didn't want to use the wrong name and give herself away. It was a clever ploy. Another thing that made me think hard was that Will stated that Annabel could have been a man or a man working with a woman. It wouldn't be too difficult to get hold of naked pictures of a beautiful woman and pass them off as yourself. Another clever ploy.

Will also mentioned that these fraudsters keep coming back for money once you have sent them some. They will make up any story to get you to give them money. They are very convincing liars and they have no shame or morals. These con artists are very sly, dishonest and ruthless. They have ruined so many people's lives. I had a lucky escape.

Short Story 6
The Magic Lamp
Page 1

I was the first volunteer in the charity shop and as I made my way to the back of the shop to put my coat and bag away, I caught a glimpse of an unusual lamp on the table. When I went to take a closer look at it, I noticed that it was a brass lamp with a large handle and a beautifully carved spout. It looked magnificent, a real antique. In fact, it looked like the type of lamp that you could make wishes with if you rubbed it. The sort that a genie came out of.

I had been working at this charity shop for over a year now and I had been very impressed with the quality of many of the items donated to the shop. Many of the women's clothes were good quality and were from shops like Marks and Spencer's, H&M and Laura Ashley. Also, there were some impressive ornaments, bric-à-brac and genuine antiques.

So, I decided to give it a rub to see what happened. I nearly jumped out of my skin when a large puff of smoke came out of the lamps spout and a huge genie appeared. He was a large, elderly man with a beard and had a bright red waistcoat and large pointy shoes that curled upwards and inwards, similar to a snake arching backwards as if ready to strike. I stood back in alarm, frightened at the sight of this apparition. He smiled and spoke quietly to me:

"Do not be afraid. I am the genie of the lamp and I will grant you three wishes," he said.

"I didn't think that genies were real. I thought you were just made up from fairy stories." I stuttered.

"Ha, Ha, we are certainly real. There aren't many of us about now though. Are you interested in making three wishes?"

"Yes. What do I have to do?"

"Firstly, you have to do three kind deeds for people you don't know. Then if you succeed you can have your three wishes," said the Genie.

"Why do I have to do these good deeds first?" I answered.

"Because I only want good people to benefit. By working as a volunteer at a charity shop you have shown you have a caring nature but you have to perform these kind acts first before you get your wishes."

"All right. What do I do when I perform these good deeds?"

"Rub the lamp again and I will appear. One final thing, you can't wish for money or wish harm on anyone."

He then disappeared into the lamp.

I bought the lamp before finishing at the shop. I got it for half price, £5, so it was a real bargain.

As I went home, I thought about what wishes I could make and what kind acts I could perform. Later I made a list of my three wishes. They were:

1. To have a book published. This would hopefully enable me to make a lot of money.
2. To buy a fairly big house, maybe a semi-detached house or detached house.
3. To find an attractive woman to be my girlfriend. She would have to have a nice figure, be caring, intelligent, unconventional, have a good sense of humour, like animals, and like reading.

After writing these items down, I sat back and thought about them. I was fairly satisfied with them so I left it.

Next, I had to think of some kind acts. I thought of visiting the local old people's home to chat to them. Perhaps I could help out at a homeless refuge. Also, I could possibly help an elderly neighbour fetch their shopping for them.

I had to call into Birmingham the next day, Sunday, to buy a few things so I could do some of these good deeds later in the afternoon.

The next day I went to the bus stop to get a bus into the city centre. While there, a middle-aged man approached me to ask me if he could use my mobile phone for a minute to ring his wife to let her know something important. His phone needed to be charged up and he was a long way from home. I am a naturally helpful person so I let him use it. I reckoned he looked honest enough. He kept his word and briefly spoke to his wife and handed it back to me. He thanked me, saying that a few other people had turned him down earlier.

It was only when he went away that I realised that this was my first good deed, without me realising it. One down, two to go.

While in the city centre, I bought all the items I needed and was heading back to get my bus home. On the way I saw some foreign tourists, looking at a map and looking puzzled. They were an American family. Many people rushed past them in a hurry and didn't offer to help.

I went over to them and asked them where they wanted to go. It was the Jewellery Quarter. They were some distance away so I offered to take them there. The American man thanked me.

On the way I spoke to them. They were a mixed-race family called Jackson from New York and they were in Britain for two weeks to look at all the sights. They had visited Birmingham for the day. Earlier they had seen Brindley Place, the New Library and Birmingham Art Gallery, which they had all enjoyed. Now they wanted to visit the Jewellery Quarter before leaving the city.

They asked me about Stratford Upon Avon, which they were going to visit tomorrow.

"It's a beautiful place," I replied, "It has all the lovely Shakespeare houses, particularly Anne Hathaway's Cottage, there are some great souvenir shops and it has a lovely river."

"We have heard so much about it. We are looking forward to seeing it," said Mr Jackson, who was a slim middle-aged black man with short black hair. He had a strong American accent.

"You could go on a tour bus which will take you to all the Shakespeare houses. This bus would also take you to the Royal Shakespeare Theatre and down by the river." I stated.

"Thanks. We might do that."

"You could buy a family ticket which won't be too much."

"Can we go on a cruise boat on the river?" enquired Mr Jackson.

"Yes, you can. I have been on them many times. It's a great way to relax and take in the scenery."

We then reached the Jewellery Quarter. The Jackson family thanked me and I left them to it.

Two down, one to go. I hadn't even planned any of these good deeds but they just came about by accident.

I set off again to make my way to the bus stop. A few minutes later a man, dressed in very old clothes, approached me for some change. I sometimes give these people a little money if I have some change on me. It depends on what they look like. He did look like he needed the money so I gave him £ 1, which was all I had on me. He seemed pleased.

On the bus home I realised I had completed all the three good deeds in one afternoon.

Later that night I rubbed the magic lamp and the genie appeared again.

He said: "Hello again. You're one of the quickest people to perform these kind acts," said the Genie.

"Yes. I did them all today without really intending to."

"These people you helped weren't there by accident. I had planned for these people to be there. You passed the test."

"What would have happened if I hadn't helped these people?" I asked.

"You wouldn't have got your three wishes. The idea is to help only kind-hearted and caring people in the world."

"I see," I answered.

So, I chose my three wishes and sure enough they all came true within one year. I got a book published that I had written, I bought a house with the earnings from the book sales and I found a girlfriend at work.

Short Story 7
Monday Again
Page 1

My alarm clock woke me up with a sudden start. I slammed down the button! For a moment I didn't realise what day it was. Then I remembered… it was Monday. I swore aloud. I hated Mondays, even though the factory I worked at wasn't too bad. Sometimes the jobs I was checking could be boring and monotonous and it did get on my nerves. I knew exactly how Bob Geldof and The Boomtowns Rats felt. I don't like Mondays. It was more like I don't like Mondays… I hate them! However, once I had got Monday over, I was all right for the rest of the week.

After checking my emails, looking at the sports news and other news and having something to eat I set off for my afternoon shift, starting at 1.30pm. Strangely enough I didn't mind the commute to work. I usually travelled by bus. I mainly read newspapers and whatever book I was reading at the time. This seemed to relax me. It got me in a reasonable mood to work.

When I reached work at 1 pm, thirty minutes before the shift started. I put my coat and bag away in the locker and went to sign in. As I was the team leader, I got ready the signing in book, the work sheets for everyone to record their checks on, gloves and pens. I would then have a chat with the morning team leader about any new jobs or problems.

Most of the time my inspectors came in on time. They were a reliable, hardworking and conscientious group of people, a mixture of men, women, English and foreign workers.

After going on my job, a GKN part that we assembled for Jaguar Land Rover, I filled out my worksheet and my rough copy sheet. I then started to inspect these parts that were assembled. The job wasn't too physically tiring. I mainly checked a few threads with a gauge and did some visual checks. I was lucky. Some factory workers had to lift heavy parts for most of their shift and they would be tired by the end of the working day and I didn't have to do rotating shifts, where I would have to be in for 6 am one week and 1:30 pm the next.

I looked around the factory. It was quite clean and well laid out. There were yellow lines where you could walk safely and other areas where you had to be careful, where there were lots of forklift trucks buzzing around like wasps around a picnic, bringing new containers of parts that needed to be assembled and taking away empty boxes. It was a busy work area.

Safety was very important at the company especially after the recent accident involving a supervisor and a forklift driver. The forklift driver had loaded up one of the lorries and was reversing backwards. The driver didn't look behind him and he reversed into the man, knocking him over and causing him to go partly under the truck. This injured supervisor had broken his left foot and broke a bone in his shoulder. He was off work for two months.

Consequently, safety was tightened up and everybody had to be very careful moving around.

As my job could be very boring and there was a fair amount of time between checks, I sometimes thought up jokes, ideas, short stories, limericks and articles for the various newsletters that I did. I also took in my rough newsletters to read through and improve. If it wasn't for these newsletters I think I would have gone crazy.

Some of the workers at the company were typical of most factories. The majority of them were nice and friendly but there was a minority of awkward workers who were difficult to work with. I learnt to avoid these awkward and unpleasant people as much as I could.

One of the worst workers was a man who worked with me assembling rear drive shafts for Jaguar Land Rover. He was called Duncan and he was rude, unpleasant, awkward and even worse, a tell-tale. I would often see him talking to one of the managers working there when they came out onto the shop floor. I quickly realised that he couldn't be trusted. I had to be careful what I said and did in front of him.

Many of my workers had problems with Duncan, including one female inspector called Eve, who had to be moved off the job she was checking for him? They didn't get on at all. Eve was a friendly, hardworking and conscientious worker so it surprised me when Duncan and Eve had problems. If Duncan couldn't get on with such a pleasant woman like Eve, who could he get on with? I had to be careful about moving Eve off the job as she was a very sensitive woman. I had to use a bit of psychology on her because she was reluctant to move. I said to her that another inspector was going on holiday for a month, which was true, and we needed a good, experienced inspector to replace him on this job, checking knuckles. I told her that she was one of my best inspectors and that I trusted her more than anyone else to do this knuckle job. It seemed to work. I didn't tell her that the line manager had asked me to move her off the job and I was planning to move her anyway.

Before Eve left that job, she had another problem with Duncan. The other inspector on the GKN Fronts was off ill so we had to get a replacement quickly. There was nobody else available who was trained up for this job so we had to get Eve back on it for the day. This caused me plenty of problems because Duncan refused to work with Eve. Normally Duncan and the other operator on fronts changed jobs every hour. I asked him if he could stay on the rears that I was checking all shift and Eve could stay on the fronts, therefore avoiding each other. He refused saying he wanted to rotate. Consequently, there was the ridiculous situation of me having to move with Duncan every time he switched jobs.

My problems with Duncan started when I was told by my supervisor that I had to have me break the same time as everyone else. As a team leader, I had my break about 15 minutes after everyone else. I got someone to cover my job at break so I didn't see a problem. I liked to have my break in the canteen later when it had less people and was much quieter. I did argue with my supervisor about this. He sympathised but because a manager had told him to do it he couldn't really refuse. My supervisor strongly hinted that it was Duncan who had reported me.

Duncan also interfered with the workers on my shift. He told me if any of my inspectors went for their break early and if they were on their phones. I was on a busy job so I couldn't always see what was going on. He even told me the exact time my inspector went for his break at 2.56 pm instead of 2.59 pm. This was on the last working day before Christmas. He couldn't even let this go. I was tempted to tell him that this had nothing to do with him and that I was the team leader but if I did, he would have gone running to one of the managers and complained about me. Our inspection company were outsiders at the factory so we weren't listened to as much as Duncan and other workers from his company.

Therefore, Duncan was getting on my nerves. I had to do something about it. I had to give it some thought. Just then Will, one of the line loaders, came up to me to talk about football.

He's a young lad, in his early twenties, about six feet tall and quite slim. He's a friendly man who liked to talk about sport, particularly football. We spoke about the weekends football results. He is a Birmingham City fan and they have been playing well recently. We also talked about the battle for the Premier League title between Liverpool and Man City. There were a few sports fans at the company so I always enjoyed talking to them when it wasn't too busy. It made this boring job a bit more bearable.

I also spoke to a few of the inspectors who worked for me. I asked them about their weekend. They had a quiet weekend like me. I liked to show interest in them as people.

They seemed a good group of people. I appreciated the good work they did for me because I have had many problems with new agency workers in the past. I remember some had walked out halfway through the shift and some had been on their phones too much. One of the most interesting inspectors was a young woman called Rachel. She was a very attractive woman, aged 22, blonde, slim with a pleasant personality, which you don't always find with a beautiful woman. She got plenty of attention from some of the younger men working there. In some ways she was similar to me, fairly quiet, caring and with a good sense of humour. We got on very well. She shared my sense of humour and started to do articles for my Newsletters. She had given me her email address so, I emailed occasionally and she sent me articles by email.

In the evening I noticed Duncan going into the office washroom. He wasn't supposed to do this. There was a sign up on the door saying only office workers allowed. I had seen him do this before a few times. It gave me an idea. He was always telling tales about other people.

Maybe someone should tell tales about him. I wrote down the exact time he went in there so it could be checked on the CCTV cameras at the company.

The problem I had was how could I report him without me getting the blame. I had to do it anonymously. I thought an anonymous phone call would be the best option for me.

Therefore, on the way home from work I stopped at a public phone box and rang the companies' number. I left a message for the office manager about Duncan always going to the staff washroom after the office staff had gone home. I reminded him that there was a notice on the door, saying 'Office staff only.' I also mentioned the time so he could check it on the CCTV. During this call I had disguised my voice as much as I could.

The next day I didn't see Duncan at work. I did ask discreetly where he was as he was due to work on the same job as me. I was told he had been suspended from work for one week without pay and given a written warning. The office manager had spoken to him when he had arrived for his afternoon shift. I tried to look surprised but inside I was pleased. It was about time this tell-tale had a bit of his own medicine.

Short Story 8

Missing Again

Page 1

Something had gone missing again. This was the third time in the last two weeks. This time it was a Christmas present for one of the volunteers, Sarah.

Elaine, the manager, questioned me about it.

"Pete, have you seen Sarah's Christmas present?" asked Elaine.

"No. Where did you put it?"

"I put it on the sorting table near the rubbish bag."

"I wonder if it's been knocked into the rubbish bag. I will have a look," I stated.

"Thanks. I will look in my office again."

So, I looked through the rubbish bag but couldn't find it. Elaine had gone through all the items on her desk but despite there being a lot of things piled up she couldn't find it either. We were both baffled by this.

We both worked in an RSPCA charity shop and there had only been two other volunteers working there apart from me. Could one of them have taken Sarah's present by mistake?

Elaine had left out Christmas presents for both of them in the same place. Surely, they wouldn't have taken the wrong present? Another reason for it going missing might have been a customer slipping into the back of the shop and taking it while we were distracted taking in bags of donations when the door was open.

Last week the assistant manager, Margaret, had lost £20. She had put £20 worth of change from her own purse in the till and taken a £20 note out. Somehow, she had mislaid it. She and another volunteer, Jane who was working at the shop at the time, looked everywhere. I wasn't there at the time so I couldn't help look for it. Nearly a week later it had still not turned up.

A few days earlier another elderly volunteer, Ada, had lost her reading glasses. She had been certain she had taken them to the charity shop that day and left them on the sorting table but she couldn't find them. All the other volunteers and also Elaine had spent ages searching for them. No luck. Even when she had gone home to look for them, there was no sign of them.

This made many of the workers at the charity shop very wary about taking anything valuable to the shop. Most people kept their mobile phones on them rather than leaving them around the shop. They also made sure they put their bags inside one of the lockers and kept it locked.

I spoke to Elaine about all these missing items.

"What do you think of all these missing things?"

"It's a puzzle. You would think that the odd thing would go missing but not four in the last fortnight," replied Elaine.

"I thought only three things went missing," I said.

"Oh. I forgot to tell you about the three cans of coke that disappeared from the fridge on Thursday," said Elaine.

"Wow. Four things. That's not normal."

"I don't want to alarm anyone but I did have my friend visit the shop on Wednesday and she is psychic. She reckons she can feel a female presence in the shop." stated Elaine.

"Do you think the shop is haunted?"

"My friend thinks it is."

"I wonder how old the shop is." I asked.

"I'm not sure but it probably dates back to the early twentieth-century."

"I think I will check the place out on the internet. There may have been a death at this place." I stated.

So later on, when I arrived home, I checked out the history of the shop. I went online and discovered that the shop had been built in 1909 and was originally a hardware shop which sold tools and appliances for the home and garden. Then in 1930 it became a book shop. A family had run this shop until 1986 when it became an RSPCA charity shop.

I continued reading facts about the shop. I sat up and took notice when I read that a tragic accident had happened in 1998. A young volunteer, a girl called Victoria, had fallen down the stairs and died. Victoria had been taking several boxes upstairs to the top store-room at the top of the shop but had lost her footing and fallen backwards. She was only 20 years old and had been working at the shop for about two years. Victoria was well liked by the Managers and the other volunteers and it was a big shock to everyone.

Consequently, the shop closed for one month while an investigation into her death was conducted. After it re-opened there were various changes to the running of the shop, regarding health and safety. Now only managers could take items up to the top store-room.

Ever since 1998 there had been the occasional sighting of a young girl. Also, items had gone missing but most people had thought they had mislaid them or lost them. This sounded familiar. I had been there for one year but I couldn't remember anything going missing before or any ghostly sightings.

I thought more about this puzzling occurrence. If Victoria had died in 1998 why is there so much paranormal activity happening now?

"Wait a minute," I said aloud.

"The girl was killed in 1998. It's December 2018 now. That's 20 years ago."

Later on, when I had eaten my tea, I went back online to find out more about Victoria. She had been slim with blonde hair and was a big animal lover. She was dedicated to helping animals. She sounded like she was a nice, caring girl.

I then read more about the last lot of ghostly sightings of the girl and missing items. It was in 2008, ten years after her death. It seemed like she made her presence felt every ten years, on the anniversary of her death.

The exact date of Victoria's death was December 2, 1998. That's why we have had the latest missing items now, although no one had mentioned seeing her.

On the next Saturday that I went to the shop, I spoke to Elaine about what I had found out about Victoria.

"So, you discovered that a young girl had died here. I didn't know that." said Elaine.

"Nor me. It seems as if this young girl Victoria appears every ten years around the anniversary of her death."

"Does she?"

"Yes, and it's the 20th anniversary of her death this month," I said.

"I think I'll have a word with my friend who's psychic to see if she can do something. I'll let you know," stated Elaine.

"Thanks. I think we need to find out why this girl keeps coming back to the shop every 10 years."

During the weekend I became more and more curious about the incident at the shop. I decided to look online for more details about Victoria's death. The local paper The Smethwick Telephone had a big front page news article about it. After reading it I was even more puzzled. It stated near the end of the article that the death was suspicious. Victoria hadn't been alone when she was taking boxes upstairs. She was with another girl called Maureen. Some of the other volunteers at the shop who had been questioned had told the police that the two girls had fallen out a few weeks before the accident and hadn't been getting on too well. One even suggested that Maureen might have pushed Victoria down the stairs. I was shocked by this.

I checked more copies of this newspaper for the next few weeks to see if there was any more news about the case but it wasn't until three weeks later that the police issued a statement.

They said that there was no evidence of any "foul play." However further on in this news report the reporter mentioned that Maureen had been interviewed about Victoria's death and had denied being near her when she fell.

I decided to tell Elaine all about this the next time I saw her at the shop, which would be in two weeks' time. Maybe Elaine might have spoken to her psychic friend by then.

When I did see Elaine the next time she told me that she and her psychic friend Valerie had visited the shop last Wednesday after it had had shut.

"What happened?" I asked.

"Valerie wondered around the shop trying to feel for any paranormal activity."

"Did she detect anything?"

"Yes. She felt a strong presence in the Top Store Room, where Victoria fell," said Elaine.

"That's interesting."

"She's going to come back another time to see if she can make contact with her."

"When will that be?"

"Maybe next week. Valerie wants to sort the problem out before Christmas," added Elaine.

"All right. Let me know what happens."

I was eager for news about this incident so I hurried off to the shop the next Saturday. After I had done several jobs, such as emptying the clothing bank, putting out some stock and giving one of the other volunteers a break on the till, I was able to speak to Elaine while we were having a break.

"How did things go with your psychic friend last week?" I asked.

"It was very interesting. Valerie actually communicated with Victoria."

"Did she? What did Victoria say?"

"She wanted to tell us that she didn't fall accidentally down the stairs. She was pushed by Maureen." stated Elaine.

"What!" I exclaimed.

"That's what she claims. That's why she has stayed here all these years and not moved on."

"What a shame. I suppose she was taking things to attract our attention."

"Yes. My friend Valerie reckons that Victoria has been doing this for a while but no one took much notice before until we did."

"Can we do anything to help her?" I asked.

"Valerie has come up with a good plan. She is going to trace where Maureen lives and speak to her," said Elaine.

"What a good idea. Can you find out where she lives?"

"I think we have a good chance. One of the old managers who worked in the shop at the time might be able to help us."

"What will you do then?" I asked.

"Valerie and me will talk to her and persuade her to come to the shop to speak to Victoria.

"Valerie wants Maureen to apologise to Victoria. Then maybe Victoria can leave this place behind and move on to the next level."

"Could Maureen get into trouble with the police?" I enquired.

"No. We won't be telling them. Victoria doesn't want her punished. She just wants an apology."

A week later when I next worked with Elaine, she told me that she had traced Maureen and that Valerie and she had spoken to her.

"That's great news. What happened?" I asked.

"We spoke to Maureen for quite a long time at her house. She is divorced with a daughter. Maureen admitted she caused Victoria's death but said it was an accident," said Elaine.

"What exactly happened?"

"Maureen told us that they had been arguing a lot that day. It was over a boy both of them liked. They had taken up some boxes to the top store room. While they were doing this they started arguing. It started to get heated and they began to push each other. They were at the top of the stairs at this point. Maureen claimed that she didn't realise they were so close to the stairs. Victoria then fell backwards and hit her head at the bottom of the stairs," explained Elaine.

"So, it could have been accidental?"

"Yes. It sounds like Maureen didn't mean to push Victoria down the stairs."

"Did she tell the police this?" I asked.

"No. She kept it from them in case she got into trouble."

"Did she not feel bad about it?"

"Maureen has regretted this all her life. She wished she hadn't done this." stated Elaine.

"It sounds a terrible tragedy."

"Maureen got very emotional and started crying. She was actually very fond of Victoria. They were very good friends until shortly before the accident. She bitterly regrets what happened." said Elaine.

"Did you ask her if she could come back to the shop?" I asked.

"Yes, we asked her to come back here and say sorry to Victoria."

"What did she say?"

"She agreed and my friend Valerie, Maureen and me came back to the shop one evening last week to try to communicate with Victoria," said Elaine.

"Did you get through to her," I said excitedly.

"It took a while. Valerie reckons that Victoria was watching us closely especially Maureen and assessing our moods. After about half an hour Valerie started to chat to Victoria. She tried to re-assure her that Maureen was very sorry about what happened and wanted to apologise."

"What happened then." I asked.

"Then Maureen stepped forward and said aloud to Victoria that she was very sorry for what she had done and that she didn't mean to push her down the stairs and cause her death. My friend Valerie then told us that Victoria smiled at hearing this and went over towards

Maureen to hug her. Of course Maureen and me couldn't see this but Valerie told us later.

"After a few minutes Victoria disappeared. She had finally gone over to the other side. We then went downstairs to have a drink in the kitchen and talked about what had happened." stated Elaine.

"So, there was a happy ending?"

"Yes. Thankfully Victoria has made things up with Maureen and moved on."

Later on, I had to take up some items to this top store room. I stood there for several minutes trying to make sense of it all. There was no sound and no movement. It was just an eerie silence. I broke the silence by saying aloud to Victoria: "I'm glad you have moved on to the next world." I listened intently for a reaction. There was nothing, which was probably a good thing. I then went downstairs to put more books out.

Short Story 9

The Nostradamus Prediction

Page 1

February 2030

Georgina was delighted by the news. She had just received an email to say she had won the Nostradamus Prize. She had accurately predicted the most technological changes that would be in use by 2030.

She thought back to ten years ago in February 2020 when she had entered the competition.

Each entrant had to successfully predict ten inventions, changes or revelations that would occur by 2030. It was a long-term competition but Georgina decided to enter it. She wasn't particularly knowledgeable about science or technology but as she liked entering competitions, she thought she would have a go. She didn't think she had a chance of winning.

Instead, she had won by getting nine out of ten innovations right. No one had got all ten of their choices right. Her nearest challenger had been a middle-aged man who had got eight out of ten correct. The prize money was £15,000, which had been donated by Sir James Dyson, the British businessman who had invented the bagless vacuum cleaner.

The nine predictions she had selected correctly were:

1. Driver-less cars, which had recently started.
2. Flying cars, which could fly or drive on the roads. The owners had to have a pilot's licence as well as a driver's licence.
3. Robot surgeons which could do simple operations.
4. A cure for dementia, particularly Alzheimer's disease.
5. The existence of UFO'S and Aliens visiting Earth will be proven.
6. Also, India's population will overtake China and become the world's most populous country.
7. People would live to be 120 years old.
8. A cure for all types of cancer.
9. Time travel. This proved to be partly right as it was only possible to visit the past not the future.

The only one she got wrong was holidays to the moon, which had been discussed many times but research had shown that not enough people were interested so businessmen didn't want to invest into this risky business proposition.

Georgina had been 30 in 2020 but she was still quite young especially as people were now living until, they were 120. Back in 2020 it was a more old-fashioned time. There were newspapers, newsagents, shops with workers on the till, cash machines, money, branches of banks and landline telephones. Most of these items and services had vanished. She missed most of these things. Progress can be a good thing but when so many good things like these have been lost, life loses a bit of its magic.

She thought about what she could spend some of this money on. There was a shop in the centre of Birmingham called 'Novelty Nostalgia', which sold products from the past. It was a little bit similar to the old shop 'Past Times' which had gone out of business. She decided to visit this shop with her friend, Emma, who was a similar age to Georgina but was smaller and had blonde hair. Emma shared a quirky sense of humour with Georgina.

A few weeks later Georgina made her way to Birmingham to meet up with her friend Emma.

On the way Georgina walked through her town of Woodham, which she had recently moved to. It was a bit depressing. There were hardly any shops now, only Aldi, Tesco, Greggs, Holland and Barrett, a chemist and one charity shop, Age UK. There weren't even any branches of banks either. The rest of the shops had shut down because so many people bought goods online now and these shops couldn't compete. Their buildings had been converted into flats, a good thing in one way because there was a shortage of places to live but also a bad thing because the soul of the town had been ripped out. These shops were the lifeblood of the town and many people now regretted abandoning them for online companies such as Amazon. In the past Georgina used to warn her family and friends not to buy so many items online because it could lead to many shops and companies going out of business. Unfortunately, most people didn't listen. They only thought of the short term, saving a few pounds.

Thankfully there were buses still around for people to get around. Driverless-cars and flying cars had recently started to become popular but there was still a need for public transport as the roads had become even more congested than ten years ago, mainly because of all the white vans delivering goods to people's homes. It was estimated that one in three vehicles on the road was delivering a parcel or package for an Amazon customer.

After meeting up with Emma in Birmingham, they made their way to the shop, 'Novelty Nostalgia.' It was situated in a part of the city called the Retro Area. This consisted of a couple of streets of shops selling old fashioned goods such as books, vinyl records, CDs, DVDs, pictures and ornaments as well as clothes, shoes and handbags.

More and more people were visiting these shops, which had old fashioned shop assistants and goods you could look at and pick up before you bought them. It was a backlash against all the online shopping that most people did these days. There was a growing market for these old types of shops. It wasn't just middle aged and older people but also young people.

'Novelty Nostalgia' was in between two charity shops, an RSPCA one and an Age UK one.

These were the only two charity shops left these days, showing peoples concern for animals and the elderly.

Georgina excitedly said, "What are you looking forward to buying?"

"I'm looking forward to buying some CDs and vinyl records," replied Emma.

"You're so old fashioned," said Georgina laughing.

"I know but I can't help having good taste."

"I'm going to browse through the book section. I want to feel a book in my hand, not a bloody Kindle," stated Georgina.

After spending two hours in this shop and buying lots of CDs, records and books they left.

"Shall we go to 'Fashion Vogue'?" said Georgina.

"Yes. I want to buy some tops and jeans," replied Emma.

'Fashion Vogue' was an old-fashioned type of women's clothes' shop selling clothes, shoes and handbags from the 1980s, 1990s, and 2000s, up until about 2020. It catered for unconventional customers who liked the old styles and fashions from the past.

After Emma had bought a few tops and a pair of jeans they both called into the RSPCA Charity shop. They were both keen on animals and liked to buy goods from this shop to help support it. They spent another hour browsing through the clothes, books, CDs, DVDs, records and bric-à-brac. They bought several items costing £10.

"Let's go for a drink," said Emma.

"All right. Let's go to Costa for a green tea."

After getting two green teas they sat down and relaxed for a while.

"How did you manage to win this Nostradamus competition?" asked Emma.

"I'm not sure. It must have been a fluke. I know I do show an interest in current affairs and news so I must have picked up some knowledge about science along the way," answered Georgina.

"You lucky sod! What are you going to spend the money on?"

"I shall save most of it, buy more things from the Retro area and also go on holiday," said Georgina.

"Where are you going?" asked Emma.

"I'm thinking of doing some time travelling, back to 2019."

"What a great idea! Can I come too?"

"Sure. I need someone to help me find my way around," replied Georgina, jokingly.

"Great. Where are you thinking of going?"

"Back to my home town of Bearwood."

"Oh Yes. That's where you were brought up. Has it changed much?" asked Emma.

"Unfortunately, it has changed, mostly for the worst. I hardly recognise it now. The only good things left are Thimblemill Library and the two lovely parks. Warley Woods and Lightwoods Park. I want to go back to when it was so much better eleven years ago."

"It had a lot more shops then, didn't it?" inquired Emma.

"Yes, it had Aldi, The Co-op, Argos, Iceland, Poundland, Greggs, Holland and Barrett, Superdrug, several banks and seven charity shops, including the RSPCA The town had a good vibe."

"I remember you liked the RSPCA shop, didn't you?"

"Yes. It was the biggest and best one in Bearwood. It had some quirky Volunteers. Let me think… Their names were… Oh yes, Sandy, Alex, Georgia, Shavy and George, stated Georgina."

"I remember them. The Managers Lynn and Rose were also very good," said Emma.

"The RSPCA shop shut in October 2019 so I want to go back to when it was still open. I have really missed it since it shut."

"I know you loved the place. You were always in it. How long is your holiday?" asked Emma.

"Two weeks, but we have to be careful not to change the past in case it affects the future. We can only observe events and things but not alter anything," stated Georgina.

"Will you be able to meet yourself?" asked Emma.

"No, I can't do that. That's why I'm going in June because in June 2019 I went on holiday to Spain for two weeks so I wasn't there at the time. I will then be able to avoid myself."

"Is it expensive?" asked Emma.

"It costs £5,000 but it will be worth it. It's not my money either. Also remember that very hot summer we had in June and July eleven years ago."

"That's right. It should be good."

"I can't wait. Roll on June 2019," said Georgina, laughing.

Short Story 10

Triskaidekaphobia
(Fear of the Number 13)

Page 1

I just knew it wasn't going to be my day when I saw the number 13 tattooed on a man's legs. I was waiting at the bus stop and I noticed this young man standing in front of me. He was wearing shorts and had numerous tattoos on both his legs. On one leg were playing cards along with the number 13. It didn't look too good and wasn't to my taste but I suppose everyone has a different viewpoint.

Halfway to work the bus broke down. Damn! The Driver asked us all to get off, saying that there was a problem with the engine. We all trooped off wearily, some of us very annoyed. I would now be late for work on my afternoon shift. I looked at my mobile phone. It was 13.13 Oh no! I hate it when I see this time.

I wondered how I had become so superstitious. It had only been in recent years. I hadn't been this bad before.

Maybe it was all the bad luck I have had recently losing my last job and my house. I just didn't like the number 13 at all these days.

I looked around at the other passengers. Most were looking on their phones. Some were talking. Then I casually counted them. There were 12, meaning there were 13 including me.

Can you believe that I said to myself?

I looked at my phone again and caught sight of the date, August 13th I had forgotten that it was the 13th. Thank goodness it wasn't Friday, the 13th. After 10 minutes the next bus came and I reached work 40 minutes late.

Surprisingly enough nothing else went wrong at work. I was relieved to finish work and was looking forward to getting home for a rest and a meal.

While waiting for my bus back into the city centre, I looked at the digital time on the bus shelter display. It was 21.13. Not again! This time my bus didn't turn up at the scheduled time of 21.11. I had a choice of waiting for the next bus in 30 minutes or walk to another bus stop for a different bus.

I decided to walk the short journey to another bus stop. It would be down a country lane with a wood on the one side. It was still reasonably light despite it being after 9 pm. At least I wouldn't be standing around waiting for another 30 minutes. I set off walking at a fairly fast pace. The weather was dry and still quite warm. It was quite a pleasant walk.

I often walked this way in the summer on my way to work as it was so pleasurable, especially walking through the wood, along the paths. The freshly cut grass, the birds singing, squirrels scampering about and the lovely old oak trees relaxed me. It was like walking through the countryside.

I decided to cut through this wood in order to save time. It would cut about ten minutes off my journey. I was quite enjoying the scenery and thinking about what meal I would have later on when I got home when I heard a blood curdling scream. I stopped in shock. It was too loud to be an animal. It sounded like a woman. I listened again… no sound.

I listened intently for about another 15 seconds. Then another loud scream. There was no mistake now. It was a woman and the noise was coming further on. I ran quickly towards the sound.

When I got nearer, I could hear voices. A woman's voice was saying, "Get off. Get off me."

I then turned a corner and saw a man on top of a woman. I shouted at him to get off. In times like these it is best to shout, swear and act aggressively. He saw me coming and he ran off quickly.

I rushed over to the woman. She was a young, black woman who was quite tall and fit. It looked like she had been jogging. Her tracksuit bottom had been pulled down but it didn't look like she had been sexually assaulted. It looked like I had arrived in time.

I then spoke to the woman to reassure her.

"Are you all right?"

"Just about," she replied shakily.

"What's your name?"

"Anna," she answered.

"Hi Anna. My name is George. Where do you live?"

"I live just across the road from the woods."

"OK. Are you all right to walk?" I asked.

"Yes. I should be all right," replied Anna.

"Good. Let's go quickly." I replied looking around anxiously.

We then started to walk fairly briskly. Luckily Anna was fairly fit. I didn't want to worry her but I was concerned that the man would return. We were under halfway through the wood so it would take us another 15 minutes to get to the end.

I tried to keep her calm by constantly talking to her and saying everything would be all right. I also asked her to phone her parents to let them know what had happened and to get them to report it to the police. She agreed. Thankfully she seemed reasonably calm.

While we walked, I could hear several rustles of leaves. At first I thought it must be some small animals, like squirrels, or birds but I kept hearing it. Something didn't feel right. It could be another person in the wood but l had a fear that it was this man who had attacked Anna.

I looked at what Anna was doing. She was walking ahead of me and was on the phone to her mom. She hadn't noticed the noises. I then thought about what I could do if he came back. I was worried. Then I had an idea. I saw a large piece of wood on the floor. I quickly picked it up and acted casually. The wood was an old tree branch that had fallen down. It was quite solid and could cause some damage. Anna hadn't noticed. She was still talking to her mom. I could hear a few things that Anna had said. It seemed like her dad had called the police and they were both waiting anxiously outside the house for her.

We probably had another quarter of a mile left to walk, about ten minutes. I couldn't believe how big this wood was. It didn't seem this big before. Then things started to go wrong for us.

The light was fading and it suddenly started to go dark. I looked at the time on my phone, it was getting on for ten o'clock. The rustling seemed to get louder and more frequent.

We still had a little way to go when I suddenly caught a glimpse of the man, who had attacked Anna, to my right. I swung around and hit him across the head with this block of wood. Down he went, moaning loudly and holding his head.

Anna looked shocked. I took her hand and told her to run with me. Thankfully she was a jogger and quite fit. I silently thanked goodness for the fact that she wasn't one of these many young, overweight women that there are around these days. If she was, I would have had to drag her along. It was my only good bit of luck today.

The man I hit was wearing a football top with the number 13 on the back. I had seen it when he fell over. Coincidence or what?

As we ran off, I looked around and saw him climbing to his feet, with blood coming down his head. He was very angry, shouting, swearing, cursing and threatening. He shouted out that he would get us.

Anna, who had been relatively calm up to then, started crying. I tried to calm her down by saying that we were near the end of the wood. She didn't take too much notice of me. I saw fear in her eyes. She had seen how nasty this man was and he was coming back for her.

I grabbed her hand and we slowly started to run. I couldn't run too fast. I was tiring but the terror in Anna's eyes forced me to carry on. We jogged on. A minute later I had to stop running when I started to gasp for air. I was 45 years old and fairly fit but I couldn't run too far. I was more of a long-distance walker. We then walked briskly.

The night was getting darker. Shadows from the trees were making our journey even more scary. For the first time I started to feel frightened. The rustling continued.

I couldn't see that clearly at all. Where was the end of the wood?

We both had to get our mobile phones out to light our way. This made the atmosphere even more eerie. On we went winding our way through the dark wood. All the sounds we heard became louder and even more scary. I could hear owls hooting but they didn't drown out the rustling. The man was getting nearer and nearer.

Even though I was feeling tired the adrenalin kept me going. The rustling got closer and closer. We were like scared animals waiting for a predator to attack. I knew now what it must be like for most animals out in the wild, the terror they must experience each day. Every sound was a threat, every smell was a potential hazard, every shadow was a danger.

Where was the exit? I then thought we had missed it and gone around in circles. I kept this to myself. Anna was still crying but was continuing to walk quickly. Had we missed the exit?

Then unexpectedly the exit for the wood appeared. We quickly walked towards it. Suddenly from nowhere the man emerged. He took a wild swing at me but I avoided it. We then rushed through the gate and across the road without looking. A bus nearly knocked us down but we carried on.

A few seconds later I heard a loud thud. The bus had hit the man. He went down as if he had been hit by a sledgehammer. I didn't look but the impact told me that he wouldn't have survived it. The bus stopped and all the passengers got out, to see how the man was. Anna's parents came running over to us. Her mom hugged Anna. The police had also arrived. Before I went over to them, I looked at the number on the bus. It was 13.

"Unbelievable!" I said aloud. "Maybe number 13 isn't so bad after all," I added as I made my way over to the police.

Short Story 11
April Fool's Day
Page 1

It was April 1st and George had got a plan to have some fun at someone else's expense.

He worked at an RSPCA charity shop on Saturdays so he was going to play up one of his fellow volunteers, Sharon, who was a 32-year-old woman with short brown hair and a medium sized figure. She was quite a friendly, talkative woman with a good sense of humour. He didn't usually like practical jokes or pranks, except for one day, April 1st.

George was usually the first volunteer in. Sharon was next in. He had brought in a joke spider he had recently found at his home when he had been cleaning up. The idea was to leave it on the floor by the lockers so she would see it when she hung her coat up.

Sharon normally came in half an hour after him, at 11 am. So, he placed it there. Linda, the manager, was working on the till so George stayed in the front store room getting some books ready to go out in the book section. Just before 11 am Sharon arrived wrapped up warmly in her big coat. She said hi to George and he acknowledged her with a smile and a good morning. He then slipped out into the back store room, pretending to get more stock out. While there he waited. Shortly after he heard a loud, piercing scream. Then more screams. He laughed and then waited a while. After composing himself he rushed out to the front store room, trying to put on his best puzzled look.

When he reached the lockers, Sharon was in a right state, pointing to the floor. "George, there's a huge spider on the floor," stuttered Sharon.

"What is it?" George asked trying not to laugh.

"There, the spider on the floor." Sharon pointed.

"Oh yes I see it," said George bending down to look at it carefully. He then picked it up by one of its legs.

"It's not real," stated George.

"What? It looks real to me."

"It's a plastic one, a joke spider. It must have fallen out of one of the donation bags," he said trying to make out it wasn't him that had left it there.

"Thank goodness for that. I hate spiders!" answered Sharon. Just then the bell rang. It was Linda asking George and Sharon to take over on the till while she took some stock upstairs.

They went into the shop and worked together serving customers. These two worked well together on the till so they always enjoyed it there.

While there George decided to play his second trick on Sharon. He told Sharon that he needed to pop out to the toilet in order to go into the back store room. He intended to make a call to the Shops phone and pretend he was someone else looking for help with an animal.

So, with Linda upstairs George made a call to the shops number. The shop regularly had people ringing up asking for advice on animal cruelty and help on abandoned animals. There was a list of numbers to give out to people.

Sharon had a liking for cats so George would ring her up about a problem concerning a cat.

He was good with accents so he put on a strong Black Country accent. He made the call.

"Hello is this the RSPCA Helpline number?" said George in an excited voice.

"No. This is a charity shop. What is the call concerning?" replied Sharon.

"It's this stray cat that has come in my house. He's violent and vicious. He's always hissing and he has scratched me."

"I'm sorry to hear this. Is he hungry?" said Sharon.

"No, he's just very violent and aggressive. Oh no he's coming towards me. Help! He's jumped up onto me and is scratching me and biting me. Can you send someone around to help me?

"Argh. Argh. Argh." shouted George.

"What's going on?" said Sharon in a panicky voice.

"Argh, argh, help me," he shouted. George then ended the call, waited a while and then went out into the shop, pretending that nothing had happened.

When he saw Sharon, she was white faced and was shaken up. She said to George that she had just had a worrying call from a man who was being attacked by a cat.

"This man phoned me to say that a cat was attacking him," said Sharon.

"That's odd," replied George, trying to keep a straight face, "What did you say to him?"

"He hung up. I think he was in a bit of trouble."

"Oh well if there is a serious problem, we should hear about it on the local news," said George.

George then went over to another part of the shop, while Sharon was serving a customer, to text a friend to come into the shop now. This was the third part of George's April fool's joke.

He had asked a friend to come into the shop to ask advice on cross dressing and buy some women's clothes to wear.

Five minutes later George's friend, Phil, appeared in the shop. He had been in a nearby shop waiting for the text to come in. Phil was tall and slim, about six feet three inches tall. Phil approached George and Sharon at the till.

"I wonder if you could help me. I am interested in cross dressing but I am new to it. Could either of you give me some advice on what type of clothes to wear." said Phil.

"Perhaps you could help him, Sharon. I can look after the till," said George. Sharon had a very puzzled and bemused look on her face but she went over to help him. George chuckled to himself.

When it was quiet George went near them to tidy up some of the clothes on the rails. He could hear some of their conversation.

"I am a size 12 shoe; can you find me a pair of high heels in this size?" said Phil in a gruff voice.

"I don't think we have any women's shoes in that size." said Sharon.

"What about bras?" said Phil.

George had to move away because he was nearly cracking up.

After about ten minutes Sharon came back to the till, looking totally baffled.

"How did things go?" George asked innocently.

"Not too bad. I gave him some advice on what to wear," replied Sharon.

"He seemed very keen. I think he must be a learner or beginner in cross dressing."

"Yes, he seemed eager to learn about what kind of clothes and shoes to wear. But he doesn't seem the type to me."

'What do you mean? said George.

"Most cross-dressing men have a strong feminine streak but he seemed too masculine," said Sharon.

"I know what you mean. He was big, about six feet three inches."

"I have had a very peculiar day, with the spider, that phone call and that learner cross dresser," said Sharon.

"Yes, it's almost like it's Friday the 13th or April 1st," said George.

"Wait a minute. It is April 1st. I had forgotten," answered Sharon.

"Oh yes, it is." George said, sounding surprised.

However, he couldn't contain himself any longer and he burst out laughing. Sharon then twigged.

"I get it. You were behind all these mad moments today. You… I will get you back!"

"I'm sorry. I couldn't help it. You must admit they were funny incidents," said George.

"They were but you have been a bit cruel," said Sharon laughing.

"You've got a good sense of humour otherwise I wouldn't have played these tricks on you," replied George.

After finishing work George said goodbye to Sharon and Linda and left for home, just a short walk down the road.

At home George texted Phil and thanked him for playing that joke. He told Phil that this was the funniest

April fool's day he could ever remember. It was hilarious.

George then went to get his paper out his bag intending to read the sports pages. However, it wasn't in there. Instead, there were other things in there… women's clothes. There were skirts, bras, dresses, tops and tights.

"Damn. That Sharon has got her own back on me." George said aloud. "She must have done it when I was on the till."

Just then Sharon texted him to say that she would return his paper later on when she was going past his house. She finished by saying, "Perhaps you could try on some of these women's clothes while you are waiting and see if they fit you. I have put some big sizes in there for you." She had got him back. George thought it was a funny response. He texted back, "Good one. I like the clothes but they aren't my colour!"

Short Story 12
My Good Luck Day
Page 1

I suppose we all have bad days, when very little goes right and many things go wrong. These are the days which we remember the most. However occasionally, very occasionally, we all have days when things go well. These are what I call 'Good Luck Days.'

Recently I had one of these 'Good Luck Days'. It started with an email from a friend who told me that he could visit Clent Hills with me next Sunday. I work on the afternoon shift so I usually check my emails before going to work. This was good news. I hadn't seen my friend for several months so it would be good to meet up with him.

On the way to the bus stop I was walking on the high street when a bird pooped a few feet from me, on my left. I was lucky there. That would have been a disaster. This must be my lucky day I thought.

On the bus I was sitting by myself on a fairly crowded bus when a very attractive woman sat next to me, wearing a short skirt and wearing one of my favourite women's perfumes, Eden.

I was reading a book at the time but I soon lost interest in it. This woman was far more interesting. My mind started wondering. I imagined going out with her for a meal, going on long walks in the park and taking her back to my place. Suddenly she looked at me and smiled as if she had read my mind. Before getting up to go she quietly said, "See you soon."

Wow! What an encounter!

At work, not a thing went wrong. I work as a Team Leader at a factory making parts for Jaguar Land Rover and sometimes there are problems with the inspectors I supervise, other workers at the company or problems with the work being made wrong. Not today. Everything went smoothly. All my inspectors turned up on time, they were all in a good mood and they all worked hard. "Why can't every day be like this?" I said aloud.

On the way home I realised it was Wednesday, Lottery night. I remembered I had put one Lotto line on and two hotpick lines on yesterday morning. Could this good luck extend to me winning a lot of money tonight? I looked forward to checking these numbers later on.

I reached into a side pocket of my bag to get my phone out and a piece of paper came out.

"What's this," I said to myself. I read it quickly. It was from the attractive woman I had met on the bus earlier. It read: "I really like you and would like to meet

up with you for a drink. Here's my number…" It was signed by Emily. How did she put it in my bag without me noticing? I must have been day dreaming.

Immediately I texted her and thanked her for giving me her number. I told her a few details about myself and suggested we meet up soon. Within half an hour she had replied, suggesting we meet up in two weeks' time at a local pub in my home town. Perfect.

It was soon my stop so I got off and walked home. Inside the door were two letters for me.

"They can't be bills, can they?" I said aloud to myself. "Surely not today." The first letter was from my credit card company, increasing my credit limit. Not bad. In fact, good news so I can help pay for my dental treatment coming up soon.

The second letter was from the Inland Revenue. "Oh no! Do I owe them money?" I asked myself aloud. Not likely. They had overtaxed me and owed me… £1,590.00. What! I re-read it several times, not taking in this large amount of money. A tax refund of nearly £1,600.

It was true. If I claimed it online, I would get it within five working days. This was like taking out a small loan without the loan repayments. It was a small fortune for me, someone who was a low paid factory worker. It was a month and a half's wages.

Can things get much better, I thought to myself. After having a shower and a change of clothes I had one of my favourite meals, salad, followed by fruit, yoghurt and chocolate.

I then rushed over to my computer to check the lotto results. Surely, I would get a big win on my 'Good Luck Day.' I quickly went on Google and put Lottery Results in the search engine.

Then the caption came up. I clicked on Lottery Results. I got my Lotto and Hotpick tickets ready to check. The numbers appeared on the screen: 5, 9, 24, 49, 54, 56.

I checked my lottery numbers… 4, 8, 25, 49, 54, 55. I swore loudly. "What the… I've got two numbers and I'm one off the other four numbers."

Then I remembered my Hotpick numbers. The low numbers looked familiar. "Got you!" I shouted. I had 5 and 9 in one of my Hotpick lines. I had missed the big one but won the small one. I had won £60 for getting two numbers. It wasn't too bad. Maybe I should call it my "Nearly Very Good Luck Day."

Short Story 13
Angry Girl
Page 1

Something didn't seem right. Greg had recently moved into a new flat at the top of the house, in the centre of his home town, Bearwood, but strange things seemed to be happening.

A week after moving in one of the pictures in his bedroom had fallen down. It had been all right for most of this first week. He had put it back up. The picture hook was still fixed to the wall. So, what had caused it to fall?

Then last night he was woken up by a light in his bedroom. It was coming from the mirror he had on the wall opposite the window. This frightened him so much that he pulled the clothes over his head. A few minutes later he looked but the light had gone. It took him a long time to get back to sleep.

The next day Greg racked his brains to think of why these occurrences had happened. It must be something to do with moving here. He had moved out of his mom's old house and this might have been the reason.

Greg believed these spooky events were connected so he decided to visit his parents grave at the weekend. In the past when something troubled him, he used to visit his parent's grave to talk over his problems. Most of the time they would be solved.

He had always believed in the afterlife and reckoned there was another 'place' that people went to after they had passed away. Maybe his mom was angry that he had left her old house.

That night Greg was woken up again, this time by a loud thud. He lay there petrified. What the hell was that he thought. He waited for a few more minutes. Then when he thought it was all over. Another loud thud! Then another loud thud! Then another loud thud! "Jesus," he shouted. "What the hell was that?" He fumbled for his torch on his bedside table and shined it shakily towards the noise. He couldn't see anything so he turned on his bedside lamp.

There were no eerie shapes or malevolent spirits, just darkness.

So, he got up and turned the light on to see more. He got a terrible shock. All his pictures had come off the wall. His George Stubbs print of a horse, the watercolour of a cottage in the country, his Van Gogh picture and also his mirror.

"What is going on here? There's something very strange happening," he said aloud to himself.

So, he put them back up on the wall. Afterwards he went to the bathroom and then went downstairs to get a drink. It was 4 am. He decided to get up. So, he had a shower, had some breakfast and then checked his emails. By then it was 8 am.

He was determined to find out the cause of all this mayhem so he set off to the cemetery to 'speak' to his mom and dad. He was on the afternoon shift so he had some spare time.

When he arrived, he asked them both what all these disturbances were about. He was respectful but annoyed. On the way he had bought some flowers to put on their grave.

Later that night there were no loud noises but he dreamt he had met his mom. She had told him that she wasn't angry he had sold her old house. She understood he had lost his job and couldn't afford the mortgage. She promised him she would investigate the problem and let him know the outcome.

When he woke, he felt much better? Hopefully these disturbances would stop. He went to put his trousers on in order to go to the bathroom but he had another big shock. His chair wasn't in the normal place by the window. Instead, his bookcase was there.

"What the hell is going on!" Greg shouted.

Then he saw that his chair was in the place of his chest of drawers. His wardrobe had also moved. The only thing that was in its usual place was his bed, which was probably too big to move and as he was sleeping in it, he would have been disturbed if it had been moved. Even his pictures had been swapped around.

He was fuming about all this because it took him half an hour to put everything back. Greg then had a shower and had a meal before setting off for his afternoon shift.

In the night, his mom came to him in his dreams again. She said that she had discovered who it was that had been bothering him? It was the spirit of a girl, called Sylvia Haywood, who had lived in his house long ago and disliked men? She had had a bad experience with one during her 'earth life' and had taken this hatred with her to the other side.

His mom had persuaded Sylvia that Greg was a good man. She had to use all her powers of persuasion to get this girl to stop. Greg's mom reckoned she had succeeded.

Greg was relieved when he woke up. "Thanks, Mom," he called out. There was no more poltergeist activity in the night so he decided to do something for this girl. He felt sorry for her. He would check online for some details about her later on.

After work Greg tried to discover some information about Sylvia. He firstly checked census reports. This proved to be very time consuming. Back he went, to 2011, then 2001, 1991, 1981 and so on. Nothing. Then further back in time until 1901. Then he found her.

"Yes!" he shouted out. She was 8 years old in 1901 but wasn't in the 1911 census. What had happened to her?

He thought about what he could do. Then a thought occurred to him. "I will check for her death certificate." He had seen this done on the television programme 'Who Do You Think You Are?' So, he checked for this online and found he could do it. He put her name into a search engine and was shocked to see that she had been murdered in 1909, aged 16. What a shame! Greg thought. No wonder she was angry.

Greg pondered on this for a long while and then came up with a plan. He would find out if she was buried in the town's cemetery, tomorrow before work.

The next day he got up early. He put some old rags and a bottle of water into a bag and then set off to the cemetery. On the way he bought some white and yellow chrysanthemums. He was taking a chance she was buried there. If she wasn't, he could put the flowers on his parents' grave.

After reaching Smethwick Old Church cemetery he looked around. It was an old churchyard, going back to the early eighteenth century. There were lots of old Ash trees and several magnificent gravestones, of angels and crosses. Greg made a start and worked quickly, going up one aisle and then going down another one. After two hours he still hadn't found the girls grave. Maybe she's not buried here he thought.

"Come on, Mom. Give me some help. I haven't got long left," he said out loud. No sooner than he had uttered these words than dozens of white butterflies appeared from nowhere.

Greg watched them as they all moved ahead of him to where he hadn't checked. He followed them and saw they had all landed on this one dirty gravestone. He rushed over to it and read the name:

SYLVIA HAYWARD
B O R N 1893
DIED 1909
REMEMBERED WITH LOVE.

He stood there silently. What a shame for her, only 16. It seemed as if no one had visited her for a long time. Her gravestone was covered with dirt and bird mess. So, he cleaned it thoroughly with some wet rags. Underneath it was still a nice gravestone. He put the flowers in front of the gravestone and stepped back to have a look at them. They looked lovely. He was glad that he had done this. It looked like someone cared for her now. He decided to visit it at the same time as his parents.

"In fact, they shouldn't be too far away. Wait a minute. It's in the same row, right at the other end. Can you believe that?" he said aloud. "This girl was so near my parent's grave all this time." He added.

When he arrived home after work, he went upstairs to his bedroom to change and get ready for a shower. There on his mirror was a message: 'THANK YOU' and a drawing of a smiling face.

Short Story 14
Alone Again
Page 1

There are times when you just feel like being on your own, away from some of the awkward people at work, your family, friends and your usual routine. Then you can do what you want without any pressure on you to do things you don't want to do. I know someone who feels like this, an old school friend called Phil, who is tired of the usual Christmases and wanted a change. He is separated from his wife and hasn't got any children so he was free to do as he wanted one Christmas, which he told me about.

He decided to do something different this year. After racking his brains, Phil thought about contacting a former workmate, Paul, he had once been friendly with. Paul had moved to Great Malvern earlier in the year. It was a very picturesque part of the Midlands with the Malvern Hills close by. He wondered if Paul wanted some company so he emailed him, asking him if it would be all right for him to stay with him for three or four days.

Later that night Paul had emailed him back. It was better news than Phil thought. Paul had decided to book a last-minute holiday to Thailand for ten days, taking in Christmas and the New Year, and he was looking for someone to house sit for him for the Christmas holiday period. "Great," Phil said aloud. He immediately emailed Paul to agree to it. Paul was due to fly out to Thailand on the Saturday before Christmas, which was on a Monday this year, so Phil had to be there by Friday night. This wasn't a problem for Phil because he could travel to Great Malvern by train from Birmingham. He texted his sister and brother to let them know that he wouldn't be seeing them this Christmas and would be staying at a friend's house.

At the weekend Phil wrote out a list of the items he would need to take, mostly the usual things in winter, several thick jumpers, a heavy coat and some walking boots for walking on the hills. In addition, he would take a few books, some seasonal DVDs like 'A Christmas Carol', 'The Amazing Mr Blunden', 'Scrooge' and 'It's a Wonderful Life.' He also wrote down a list of some of his favourite food, including fruit, vegetables, yoghurts and chocolate.

Soon it was time for Phil to travel to Great Malvern. He collected his large bag and set off for his train. A couple of hours later his was at his friend Paul's house, an eighteenth-century detached house down an old part of the town in a cul-de-sac. It had five bedrooms, a very large living room and a spacious kitchen. The house was one of only four houses in the road. It had a lot of privacy but it was still only five minutes' walk to the shops. Almost a perfect location.

Paul warmly welcomed him. He was a similar age to Phil but was more overweight and looked older than his age. He showed Phil around the house, pointing out various things to him. Phil's room was a double room with a very comfortable double bed. He had a good view of the hills from his bedroom window.

Afterwards Paul sent out for some pizza takeaways for them both. They then reminisced about the old days when they worked at a company called Frays. Paul stated that he couldn't stay up too late as he had to be up at 6 am to get a 9 am flight from Birmingham airport.

Paul did say that Phil could have the freedom of the house except for his bedroom, which he would lock.

The next morning Phil decided to explore the house and garden. The living room contained a modern, flat screen television with lots of terrestrial, satellite and streaming channels. Also, there was a DVD Player for him to play his DVD'S that he had brought up for the evenings.

The kitchen was spacious and had a large fridge which Phil had put most of his vegetarian food, cheese, yogurts and so on inside. The garden was long with several flower beds but as it was winter, he wouldn't be sitting outside in it.

When he explored the front room, he was delighted to find three large bookcases, about four feet high. Like Paul, Phil had always been interested in books. There were books about the paranormal, all kinds of sports books, biographies, autobiographies, poetry books, classic novels and modern novels, just the kind of books Phil liked. He picked a few out to read later.

After lunch he went on the Malvern Hills for a long walk. The weather was dry but cold so he put his warm coat and gloves on. He spent three hours on the hills, marvelling at all the beautiful countryside. Malvern Hills are 8 miles long and over 1400 feet high at its highest point. They have inspired writers such as J.R.R Tolkein and C.S Lewis and the composer Sir Edward Elgar. While he was walking, he thought about his friend Paul. He had always been clever and very ambitious so it didn't surprise him that he had been successful and had bought such an expensive house in a lovely part of the country. In the evening he watched a wildlife DVD he had brought up and read some of the book he was reading.

When Phil got up on Christmas Eve after having a good night's sleep he emailed Paul to let him know that everything was all right. He added that he had settled in quite well and was enjoying the peace and quiet of the house.

In mid-afternoon, after having a lovely meal of salad, fruit, yoghurt and chocolate, Phil went on another walk on Malvern Hills. He thought how lucky Paul was to live so close to such a beautiful place. The weather was still very cold. He did speak to a friendly man, he met on the hills, who lived locally who said there was snow on the way and it might be a white Christmas. This set him thinking. He decided to check the weather forecast later. He continued walking on the hills for another two hours, observing the beautiful scenery. There were plenty of other people there, most walking on their own and some walking their dogs. He set off for home at around 4.30 pm as it was getting dark.

Before going home, he had a walk through the pleasant town of Great Malvern. It has a splendid church, three excellent pubs and several good shops. He thought he would try one of the pubs in the next few days.

Later on, he watched some television programmes and also watched the weather forecast for Christmas Day and Boxing Day. He was shocked to find that heavy snow was predicted for Boxing Day.

Christmas Day was also dry but much colder than recent days, probably about five degrees. After Phil had had a late breakfast of fruit and yoghurt he went out for another long walk on the hills. This invigorated him and made him feel good, similar to when he had a shower or bath. It was like having an internal shower.

On his way back he looked at the side of the house and noticed how much longer it looked than when you were inside. He decided to investigate. He went into the front room and thought that it didn't look that big. A thought suddenly occurred to him. Many old houses have secret panels which hide things away. He looked at the end wall, which had a large bookcase on, and tapped on the wall. There was a hollow sound. So, he carefully pulled the bookcase out so he could see behind it and immediately saw a rusty lever. After pulling it, the wall opened inwards, revealing a long passage which he followed for about ten metres. A door was at the end of this passage. It had an old lock with a large key inside. He turned the key. Phil stepped outside and saw that it led to an alley. He followed it until he reached two paths, one went to the town centre and the other was at the bottom of the hills. This was a surprise; it was a short cut to the town and hills. It would save him a five-minute walk. He decided to go this way the next time he wanted to go to the hills.

He went back inside, locked the door, put the key back in the lock and went back into the front room. He left the bookcase away from the wall to make it easier to go out down the secret passage. This puzzled him, what was the purpose of this secret passage? Was it just a shortcut to town and the hills?

Later on, Phil enjoyed a pleasant Christmas meal, watched several Christmas television programmes and also watched some of his DVDs. Even though he was on his own he had an enjoyable time. He could do what he wanted.

On Boxing Day morning when Phil awoke, quite late at 11 am, he looked out the window and saw that it had snowed quite heavily. It looked quite deep. Following a quick shower and a quick breakfast he put on his coat and gloves and went out through the secret passage, out into the cold day to investigate. By now it was nearly midday but the snow was still coming down heavily. He had always enjoyed snow so he decided to go out walking in it for a short while.

Phil struggled through the deep snow. It was like trying to walk in water, he wasn't going too far. As he climbed up, he saw a right turning and there were two people there, a man and a woman. The woman was sitting down in some distress and the man was crouching beside her. Phil rushed over to them and asked them what had happened.

"My girlfriend slipped in the snow," the man answered.

"What's your name?" said Phil.

My name is Mike. My girlfriend's name is Eva.

"Hi, I'm Phil. Is Eva badly hurt?"

"She slipped and fell badly. I think she has twisted her ankle. She can't walk."

"I live quite close by. Do you want to come back to my place? I'm staying at my friend's house while he's on holiday." said Phil.

"Thanks. That's good of you. We have rung for an ambulance but as there is so much snow, they can't get through to the town yet."

"OK. If we both support Eva, we should be able to get her back to my place."

So, between them Phil and Mike managed to support Eva and carry her down the hill slowly and steadily, not going too quickly in case they fell. The snow was still coming down thick and fast. Eventually after half an hour they reached Phil's place. Soon Eva was sitting down on the settee.

"How are you feeling Eva?" asked Phil.

"A bit better now I am sitting down. I can't put any weight on my foot," said Eva.

"Shall I get you both a drink?"

"Yes, that would be nice. Two teas please, milk and no sugar," replied Mike.

"All right. I will fix you both drinks. I also want to have a look at how bad the weather is."

So, after getting Mike and Eva drinks, Phil went out into the snow to see how bad the weather was. The snow was still heavy and was getting deeper and deeper. He thought that there would be no way an ambulance could get through. He walked through the town centre.

No one was about. He decided to check on his neighbours. There were only four houses in the road. Most were young couples but there was one elderly widower who Paul had mentioned.

He lived at number 5 so Phil knocked on his door. It took him several minutes before he answered. He was wearing a blanket around his shoulders.

"Hello, I'm Phil who is house sitting for Paul at number 4. I've just called to see how you are."

"Hello Phil. My name is Frank. I'm not too good really. My boiler has packed up and I don't have much heating."

"Have you another fire?"

"Yes, but it's only a small two bar electric fire. It's not warm enough. I'm having to wear lots of extra clothes and have a blanket," replied Frank.

"I see. Why don't you come and stay at my house? The central heating is on and it's lovely and warm."

"Are you sure. I don't want to impose," answered Frank.

"No, you won't be. I can't let you stay here," replied Phil.

Phil took Frank next door and showed him to the living room where Mike and Eva were. He introduced them to Frank and explained what his situation was. It looked like Phil had company for a few days. Phil made everyone a drink as well as himself and then sat down to discuss with them what they could do.

"The snow is very deep at the moment and it looks like you might all be here for a while, are you all right to stay here? You are all welcome," said Phil.

"Yes. Thanks for the offer. Eva and me appreciate it," said Mike.

"What about you Frank?"

"Thanks for the offer. I think it would be too cold for me to stay at my place. I won't be able to get the boiler fixed until all this snow goes."

"Now there are five bedrooms. Four are upstairs and one downstairs. Mike, can you and Eva have this ground floor bedroom?" Phil asked.

"Yes, that should be fine."

"Thanks. I should be all right as long as I don't have to climb stairs," stated Eva.

"That's good. There is a downstairs bathroom as well. Frank, can you have one of the spare bedrooms upstairs?"

"Yes. That all right. I'm a bit stiffer these days but I can still climb stairs."

"So that's everyone sorted. There's plenty of food in the kitchen for us all as well," said Phil.

"Can we check the weather forecast? I want to see if there is more snow due for tomorrow," said Eva.

"All right I will put the telly on. The news should be on soon. We can check the local news and weather forecast," Phil said.

They watched the national news, local news and finally the weather forecast. The news wasn't good. The weather was going to remain very cold, at 0-5 degrees centigrade for the next few days. There was more snow forecast for tomorrow. Even in a few days' time it would still be very cold with more snow showers.

"It looks like the weather will be bad for the next two or three days. You will all have to stay here until the snow clears away."

"Yes, it seems like our best option," stated Mike.

"As long as you don't mind us staying here," said Frank.

"It should be all right. I have had three days on my own which is what I wanted. but I don't mind a bit of company now," said Phil. Just then the doorbell rang. It was a middle-aged couple from number 3, Ivan and Dawn.

They told Phil that their pipes had burst and had flooded their downstairs rooms. They had cleaned up but it would take a few days to dry out. They asked Phil if it would be all right for them to stay at the house.

Phil invited them in. It looked like his plans for a people free Christmas had ended. Strangely enough he wasn't that disappointed. He would have to email Paul later to let him know what had happened. He wondered what Paul would make of it.

Short Story 15
The End
Page 1

I suddenly feel this intense pain on the left side of my chest. It cuts right through me. What's happening! Next, I collapse on the floor and pass out.

Then I find my life is flashing before me very quickly, similar to when you wind on a DVD of a film. I see myself as a young boy with my family, going to school, playing with my brother in the back garden, starting my first job, going out with my first girlfriend, Diane, all the way up to me collapsing.

Darkness then envelops me. I'm travelling down a long, dark tunnel. There's a small light at the end of it. I don't know how long this tunnel is but it takes some time before I reach the end.

I try to resist. I try to call out that I don't want to go down this tunnel but no sound comes out my mouth. There is no noise at all. It's eerily silent.

I eventually reach the end of the tunnel. I find myself outside in a beautiful field. It's a bright sunny day. There are trees, meadows, rivers, streams and hedges. It's lovely countryside and it stretches for miles. There's not a house in sight. Then in the distance I see people coming towards me. I strain my eyes to try to recognise them. As they approach me, they look strangely familiar but I can't recall who they are. There are six people, all quite young.

Then they smile at me and call my name. I then recognise two of them. One is my mother and the other is my father. They look younger than I remember them.

"Mom, Dad, it's you, it's great to see you again," I say.

"Yes son, it's your parents and also your Great Grandparents," replies Mom.

"Dad, you look so slim."

"Are you saying I was fat before?" says Dad laughing.

"Sorry, I didn't mean to be rude," I say.

"I know son, I'm only joking."

"What is this place? Is it heaven?" I ask.

"We don't have much time to explain things now. We shall tell you more soon," says Mom.

"Am I dead?"

"Yes, you are," replies my dad.

"Can't I have a bit longer? There are more things I want to do in life."

"I'm sorry but it's not our decision. There's one thing you must do immediately," says my mom.

"What's that?"

"You have to go to your own funeral," says my mom.

Before I can respond I find myself at Smethwick Old Church, where my dad is buried. It's an imposing but plain eighteenth-century church with some fine stained-glass windows. It's a grade 2 listed building and is the oldest building in the town. It also has a tranquil churchyard with several beautiful gravestones, many with large crosses.

Inside the church I can see most of my family at the front of one side, my sister, Sue and her family and my brother, Mike. There's also my uncle, aunt and three cousins. On the other side of the church there are many of my friends, workmates and fellow workers at my former charity shops: The RSPCA and The British Heart Foundation. I stand and watch them from the back.

It's sad to see all these people who mean so much to me. I won't be able to see them, speak to them, joke with them or go to places with them I like such as Malvern Hills, Stratford Upon Avon and my local park, Warley Woods.

Music suddenly starts up. They all then start to sing a hymn, 'Jerusalem' by William Blake. The lovely melody moves me to tears. It's always been a favourite hymn of mine. The song has often been played at England cricket games so it has good memories for me.

A year ago, I had reluctantly made a will. I had left the modest amount of money to my family, mainly my sister, her family and my brother. I had also mentioned what I wanted at my funeral, the hymns, poems and songs and that I wanted to be buried with my father.

The Vicar starts to read a poem I had requested. It's 'Remember' by Christina Rossetti.

Remember me when I am gone away,
Gone far away into the silent land;
When you can no more hold me by the hand,
Nor I half turn to go yet turning stay.
Remember me when no more day by day
You tell me of our future that you plann'd:
Only remember me; you understand
It will be late to counsel then or pray.
Yet if you should forget me for a while
And afterwards remember, do not grieve.

I have always liked this sad but moving poem. This was also read at my mom's funeral many years ago.

This Vicar also recites two Shakespearean quotes that I like. The first is "We can't hold immortality's strong hand." The second one is: "We are such stuff as dreams are made on, and our, little life is rounded with asleep." These Shakespearean quotes about death are quite fitting.

I 'm staggered to find that one of my friends, Roger, reads a tribute to me. He mentions the time when I helped him through a very tough time in his life when he was out of work and struggling to make ends meet. He says that I was the only person to help him. I'm really moved and touched by this.

Another tribute to me is from Rebecca the manageress of the British Heart Foundation charity shop that I have worked at for nearly four years. She states how hard I used to work at the shop and how reliable I was, never having any time off work despite not being paid. These two tributes make me sad but also proud that I had made a good impact on people's lives.

The service finishes with another of my favourite hymns:

The Lord Is My Shepherd.

Shortly after the end of this lovely hymn my coffin is carried out to the music of my favourite band The Beatles. It's an appropriate song, 'In My Life.' I watch the undertakers as they carry me out to the grave where my father is buried.

I suddenly leave the church and I'm back in what I think is heaven with my mom and dad.

My four great grandparents are not there.

"How are you son?" asks my dad.

"I'm a bit dazed. I 've just been to my funeral. I can't take it all in."

"It's upsetting but you need to attend your own funeral," adds Dad.

"Why's that?" I ask.

"It's a way of ending your previous life. You have to say goodbye to all your family, friends and workmates, like closure," says Mom.

All three of us start to walk through this beautiful field, talking while we do so.

"Can you tell me more about this place, Mom?" I ask.

"All right. It is a form of heaven, where everyone who dies goes to so their life can be evaluated."

"What happens now?"

"The family elders will assess your life and see if you can move onto the next spiritual level."

"Can I ask you a question, Mom?"

"Yes. What is it?"

"Does it ever rain here?"

"No," replies Mom.

We then reach the first building I have seen since I have arrived in heaven. It's a very large thatched cottage with small windows and rose bushes around the door. There is also a large garden in the back full of colourful flowers. "What a lovely place," I remark.

"Yes. It's a visualisation of your ideal house," said Dad.

"How did they know that?" I ask.

"They know everything."

"Who are they?" I ask.

"You have seen them already," says Mom.

"You mean my great grandparents?"

"Yes. They are the family elders. They will decide your future," says Mom.

We then enter the beautiful house. It is even better inside, well decorated with lime green walls to aid calmness, old Victorian furniture and many pictures on the wall. It is just like a house I would have. There is a large table in the dining room with lots of chairs. We all sit down. I am next to Mom and Dad. After looking around I notice a big screen. Shortly after my great grandparents come in the room. My great grandfather speaks first:

"When we assess someone's life, compassion is one of the first qualities we look for in a person. We look at whether he or she has behaved well towards other people and also animals during their life. This can be shown by them doing small acts of kindness towards their elderly neighbours, helping family and friends when they are in trouble or working for charities."

"Firstly, I want to ask George to evaluate his own life. Please stand up and speak, George," said my great grandfather.

I am surprised by this. I reluctantly get up and stand nervously for a while. I have never been too confident of speaking in public. I clear my throat and say:

"I don't think I have achieved much in life. I have mostly worked in factories and not fulfilled my potential."

Then my paternal great-grandfather speaks. He is fairly complimentary about me:

"I have assessed your life and I have come to the conclusion you are ready to move onto the next life. You have achieved more in your life than you realise. You have helped many people in trouble and have shown a lot of compassion. Another thing you have achieved is that you have written a book that has influenced many people. You can now move onto the next spiritual plane. Your parents will join you later. Now is there anything you would like to do before moving onto the next plane?"

"Yes. Can I visit some of the places from my old life?" I ask.

"Yes, you can do this if you want. All you have to do is think of the place. Then you will go there." said my great grandfather.

So, I think of my childhood home in Capethorn Road, Smethwick, where I lived with my mom, dad, sister and brother. Immediately I am back in the past in the same house my family lived in during the 1970s. Some of the house was how I remembered it but there were things I had forgotten. I hadn't remembered the type of wallpaper we had or the colour of the furniture. I did remember the cosy living room, the large settee, the two armchairs, the small black and white television and the coal fire. It was basic but it was comfortable.

I thought of all the television programmes we used to watch in the living room, particularly on Saturday evenings. Firstly, we watched Dr Who, then The Generation Game, The Two Ronnies, Match of The Day and finally Parkinson. It was great programme after great programme. On Sunday night it would be The Golden Shot, All Creatures Great and Small and That's Life, all good entertainment shows.

I also look around the small kitchen. This was where my dad used to listen to football games and boxing matches on the radio while he had his supper. I would often be in there with him.

Outside there was the small garden, two flower beds each side separated by a slabbed path. Mom used to spend so much time planting flowers and tending to this garden.

Another thing I remembered were all the games that my brother Mike and I used to play in the garden, football and cricket. We used to regularly lose our balls over the neighbours' fences into their gardens. Then I would have to climb over their fences at night to retrieve them. This used to happen nearly every night at the weekend or in the school holidays. They were good times.

Before going back inside I look at the outside toilet. We had this until I was about 14 years old. Then we had an indoor one fitted in the bathroom. This outside toilet looks grim.

I have a look around my old bedroom which I used to share with my brother. We both had single beds. Also, in the bedroom were a wardrobe, a bedside table and a chest of drawers.

This bedroom was my haven when I wanted to get away from the rest of the family and be by myself. Sometimes I would read up there or just lie on my bed thinking.

I finally leave the house and walk up the road. It looks so small now, only 50 houses in the road. As I walk up the road, I try to remember all the neighbours who lived in these houses.

At the top of the road is another place that brings back good memories for me – the local sweet shop. This was where my sister Sue, brother Mike and I used to go to buy sweets, chocolate crisps and pop. The shop was owned by an elderly woman and her middle-aged daughter. We were always in there spending our pocket money. They were good times.

Finally, I visit my old library, Thimblemill Library, where my sister, my brother and I used to go to borrow books. We were all big readers when we were young and we would borrow three books each read them and then swap them for each other's book.

Suddenly I am back in heaven with my parents and great-grandparents. Like an actor whose performance has just ended, I need to leave the stage. Next, I see them all smiling and waving as I ascend upwards. I land on another plane. This is the next chapter in my life. I hope it will be as good as my last one.

9 781035 870462